PRAISE FOR *HELL TO PAY*

"I haven't read all of Andy's books, but I've read several, and I like that he writes whatever he likes. He's got some damn good stuff."

—Joe R. Lansdale, author of *Cold in July*

"Rausch's writing is like a serpent. It's lean. It's clever. It coils around you...and then it strikes. It's glorious, but be warned—there is no anti-venom."

—Chris Miller, author of *Dust*

HELL TO PAY

ANDY RAUSCH

HELL TO PAY

A Diggy and Stick Crime Novel

DOWN & OUT
BOOKS

Down & Out Books
3959 Van Dyke Road, Suite 265
Lutz, FL 33558
DownAndOutBooks.com

Cover design by Zach McCain

ISBN: 1-64396-248-5
ISBN-13: 978-1-64396-248-1

PROLOGUE

The former cops, Diggy and Stick, one black, one white, were looking around the toy store, pretending to be interested in toys. What they were really doing, however, was watching the little black girl, Tiffany, staring at Barbie dolls, Barbie cars, Barbie houses, and lots of other Barbie shit.

They had followed her into the store. The two men had been checking in on her for the past year, but they'd never actually been this close to her. Knowing Tiffany had lost her drug dealer daddy, they did their best to make sure the little girl never went without.

As the two middle-aged men stood down the aisle, feigning interest in a stuffed unicorn, trying to sneak glances at the little girl without looking creepy, which was no mean feat, mind you, Stick said, "You think she's been getting the cash we send her mother?"

Diggy turned past Stick, taking inventory of Tiffany's clothing, shoes, and backpack. "Maybe some. I mean, her clothes look alright. Not name brands, but decent."

Stick looked at Diggy. "You think her mother spends it on herself?"

Diggy nodded. "She's probably on something. Most likely meth."

Looking over the fluffy white and pink unicorn Stick was holding, they saw Tiffany pick up a pink Barbie convertible. She

1

stared at it longingly. Diggy looked at Stick and nodded his head toward Tiffany. They both turned and headed her direction.

When they were about four steps away, Diggy said, "Hey, little girl."

Tiffany turned toward them, sizing them up warily.

Diggy turned on his charm. "I got a niece who's about your age."

"I'm eight," Tiffany said.

This was Diggy's opening. "My niece is eight too!"

The little girl's face lit up.

"So maybe you can help me," Diggy said.

The little girl just stared at him.

"My niece likes Barbie, too," Diggy said. "'Cept I don't know what to get her." He paused. "How about you? What do you like?"

The little girl looked down at the boxed convertible she was holding.

"I like this," she said.

Diggy smiled. "Ooh wee, that is a beaut." He turned toward his partner. "Don't you think so, Stick? Ain't she a beaut?"

"She is a beaut," Stick said. "That's a nice car."

"How about you?" Diggy asked the girl. "You gonna buy it?"

When he asked this, her face fell. "Well," she said, "I like it, but I don't have any money."

"Don't you get an allowance or somethin'?"

"Nah. Mama says we ain't got money for toys."

"Damn," Stick said. "That's a shame."

Diggy dug into his pocket. When Tiffany turned back toward the car, he dropped a crumpled twenty onto the tile floor.

"*Heyyy,*" Diggy said. "Looky what I found."

The little girl looked at him, saw where he was looking, and spotted the money. Her eyes lit up and she looked up at him.

"You musta dropped that," he told her.

The little girl looked back down at the bill.

"No," she said, shaking her head. "That ain't mine."

"Well, it ain't mine, neither," Diggy said. "And you know what they say."

The little girl stared at him.

"Finders keepers," Stick said.

The little girl looked at Diggy. "You found it, though, so that means it's yours."

"Nah," Diggy said. "It's closer to you, so I think you oughta take it."

The little girl's eyes went from Diggy to the money, and then back to Diggy again.

"Are you...*sure?*" she asked.

Diggy nodded.

"Hell yes," Stick said.

"Now you can buy yourself that car you got there," Diggy said.

As the little girl lowered herself to pick up the money, the convertible still under her other arm, she said, "I would, but it's not enough."

"It ain't?" Diggy said. "Well, how much is it?"

Now standing erect again with the money in one hand and the convertible in the other, Tiffany said, "Thirty-four ninety-nine."

"Huh," Diggy said, digging into his pocket again. Then he turned to Stick and whispered, "That's all I got."

Stick reached into his pocket and fished out a twenty and dropped it on the floor. Tiffany watched him do it, and he said, "Oh look, more money!"

Tiffany eyed them suspiciously.

Diggy leaned down to her eye level. "We gon' leave, maybe come back and get my niece's present later." He winked at her. "So for now, you best pick up this money and buy yourself the car."

CHAPTER ONE

Stick was five drinks past drunk when he saw his raven-haired ex and her new boyfriend sitting in a booth across the bar. The Bee Gees' "Night Fever" was playing on the jukebox for the third straight time. "Some motherfucker done played this shit over and over again," Diggy said. But Stick didn't hear him; his eyes were locked on Tina and Keeling. When Stick didn't comment on Diggy's observation, Diggy followed his eyeline, now seeing them himself.

"Ah shit, Stick," he said. "I know what you thinkin'."

Stick didn't take his eyes off the couple. "Of course you do."

"We don't need no trouble, Stick."

Stick didn't comment. He just kept staring.

"Ain't none of it gon' bring her back," Diggy said.

Stick just stared in silence.

"Lemme ask you something," Diggy said.

Stick turned and looked at his friend. "What?"

"If it was any other motherfucker with her…anybody other than that peckerfucker Keeling, would you still be this mad?"

Stick grinned a little, a spark in his eyes. "Probably not." He looked back at Keeling and his ex-wife. "Don't get me wrong, I wouldn't love it, but that guy…"

Diggy looked across the room at Keeling. "That dude is trash."

"He's worse than trash. I never liked him."

"Me neither."

"I knew he was trouble from the moment I saw him."

Diggy nodded. "You said."

"You're right, I did," Stick said. "And, as it happens, I was right."

Diggy took a drink of his scotch. "For once, you was right."

Stick turned and looked at Diggy.

"So what you gon' do now?" Diggy asked.

Stick's grin widened. "I'm going to drink the rest of my drink."

"Then what?"

"I'll let you know when I'm done." Stick raised his glass, held it toward Diggy in salute, and downed it in one gulp. He set the empty glass down on the table and went back to staring at Tina and Keeling.

"Now what?" Diggy asked.

Stick looked at him. "You already know, brother. You already know."

Diggy sighed. "Don't do this, man."

Stick rose up from his chair and stood in place, staring at Keeling, hoping the prick might see him standing there, but he didn't.

"I'll be back," Stick said, heading for their table.

"Like hell," Diggy said. "If you're goin', I'm goin'. I'm not lettin' your sorry white ass get beat up without backup."

Diggy expected Stick to laugh or at least acknowledge the humor in his reply, but Stick was too far gone. Stick sauntered over toward the couple.

"Good Christ," Diggy muttered, a few steps behind.

Tina was the first person at the table to see Stick approaching. She and Keeling were sitting with Keeling's partner, another knucklehead cop named Jenks, and Jenks's blonde wife. Tina's eyes got big and a fire came into them the moment she laid eyes on her ex. Before Tina could speak, and before anyone else at the table saw him, Stick spoke. "How the fuck are ya, Keeling?"

When Keeling saw Stick, he visibly tensed. Jenks's chest immediately puffed out. Before either cop could say a word, Tina said, "Goddammit, Stick, just leave us alone."

Stick was right up against the table now, his eyes locked on Keeling's. "It's not you I want to talk to, Tina. I want to talk to Mr. Piece-of-Shit Lover Boy here."

Keeling started to stand, but Stick put his hand on the cop's shoulder and pushed him back down into the booth.

"You'd better watch yourself!" Jenks warned.

"Shut your mouth, you dumb shitkicker," Diggy said from behind Stick. "This ain't none of your business. This is between Stick and your fuckhead partner."

"If it ain't none of my business, then it ain't none of yours either."

"That's right, it ain't," Diggy said. "But I'm gonna make sure Stick don't get bum-rushed. Keeling is a man...well, sorta, so they can fight it out themselves without help from us."

Keeling looked up at Stick, trying his best to act indifferent. "That what you want, Stick? You wanna fight?"

"I'm not here to be your butt buddy," Stick said. Then he looked at Jenks. "That's his job."

Jenks tried to get up, but he was pinned in against the wall with nowhere to go.

"You better sit your ass down, Jenks," Diggy warned.

Jenks begrudgingly settled back into the booth.

"You know what?" Stick said. "How about we just let bygones be bygones? What you think about that?"

Keeling looked up at him with a look of suspicion.

"I'm serious," Stick said. He reached down and grabbed Tina's drink, a glass with some fruity pink shit in it. "You mind, Tina?"

"Goddammit, Stick," she said.

Stick held the glass out toward Keeling. "Pick up your glass, pal. You and me, we're gonna have a drink together."

Keeling just stared at him with a confused look on his face.

Stick used the glass of pink shit to motion toward Keeling's beer. "I'm serious, Keeling. Raise that shit up and have a drink with me. It's the least you can do."

Keeling stared at him for another moment, and then hesitantly wrapped his hand around his beer bottle.

"There you go," Stick said. "Just like that."

"This don't mean we're gonna be friends," Keeling said.

"You tryin' ta hurt my feelings?"

Keeling was starting to raise his beer when Stick's arm shot forward, jamming his drink into Keeling's face, shattering the glass. Keeling recoiled and dark red blood immediately sprouted up from his eyebrow and beside his eye.

"*Dammit, Stick!*" Tina shouted.

Keeling remained recoiled for a moment, stunned, but Jenks had his hands out, reaching for Stick, trying to climb up over his injured partner. His hands were close to Stick's arm when Diggy shoved Stick aside, pushing his way in and connecting a hard right to Jenks's forehead. Jenks flailed back, his head bouncing off the wall like a pinball off a flipper.

Chaos erupted around them. People started screaming and there was a frantic commotion. "Night Fever" was replaying on the jukebox for the fourth time. Keeling had snapped back and was shaking off the blow, climbing to his feet now. The moment he was standing, Stick connected with a hard uppercut to his jaw, knocking him back into the booth onto Jenks.

Jenks, Jenks's wife, and Tina were all screaming obscenities at Stick.

Stick stood there staring at them, ready to fight any one of them. "*Shut the fuck up, all of you!*"

Before anyone could respond, Stick felt a hand gripping his shoulder. He spun with his fist up and saw it was Diggy.

"Come on," Diggy said. "We gotta go."

"Bullshit," Stick said, turning back toward Keeling.

"*I've called the cops!*" a man yelled from behind them.

"Then I'd better make the most of the time I've got," Stick said, grinning. He dove into the booth on top of Keeling. There was a flurry of arms and legs, like an old-time cartoon, as Stick punched Keeling, Keeling punched Stick, and Jenks reached around Keeling to punch Stick but inadvertently punched them both.

Tina sat across the table with her arms crossed, looking pissed. She looked up at Diggy, who stood and watched. "Dammit, Diggy," she said. "Why do you let him do this?"

Diggy looked at her and grinned. "You was married to him for a long-ass time. You should know better than anybody that there ain't no stoppin' Stick. If he gets it in his mind to do something, he gon' do it."

Tina sighed. "Ain't that the fuckin' truth." She raised a cigarette to her lips and lit it, seemingly oblivious to the scuffle across the table.

CHAPTER TWO

When the cops arrived—the ones on duty—it was Ballantine and Perez, whom Diggy and Stick both knew and hated. The cops looked at Diggy and Stick's bloody knuckles. Then they looked at their comrades' swollen, beat up faces, and they knew the score. As they escorted Diggy and Stick out of the bar in cuffs, Ballantine and Perez cracked jokes.

"I see you still got a mean right," Ballantine said to Stick.

Perez chuckled and Ballantine said, "Did you know Stick here used to be a fighter?"

Perez looked at him, blinking. "What, like a boxer or somethin'?"

"Not exactly," Ballantine said. "He used to do bare knuckle brawling in parking lots of shitholes like this."

"I actually fought here a couple times," Stick said dryly.

Diggy chuckled. "Yeah, you did. You beat the hell out that big Filipino."

"Oh yeah, him," Stick remembered. "I hated that guy."

"More than you hate Keeling?" Ballantine asked.

Diggy chuckled, and Stick said, "Not even close."

The two cops positioned Diggy and Stick against the side of the cruiser, making them place open palms against the side of it, saying they had to check them for weapons.

"The only weapon I got is my fists," Stick said.

"And the only weapon I got is this big ol' dick," Diggy said.

The cops chuckled as they patted them down. When Perez's hand came up under Diggy's crotch, Diggy said, "Yep, there it is, in all its python glory."

"Don't seem all that big to me," Perez said.

"Ya mama sees it different," Diggy said.

Perez stood up and took a step back. *"Hey!"*

"No, really. I'm your daddy, Perez. Just ask that bitch."

"You're about the same age as me, dickhead," Perez snarled.

Diggy grinned. "What can I say? I had an early start."

Perez stepped forward like he was about to strike Diggy, but Ballantine intervened. "Cool it."

"Nobody talks about my mama."

"Diggy did," Stick said.

"My mama is a good woman!"

Diggy said, "Fuck your mama."

Perez's light-skinned Hispanic features reddened with anger.

"Just put his smart ass in the car," Ballantine said.

Ballantine opened the cruiser's back door and ushered Stick in. When Perez assisted Diggy into the car, he made a point of banging Diggy's head against the top of the door frame.

"Fuck!" Diggy yelped.

"Was that 'cause he's black?" Stick asked mockingly.

"No, it's because he's an asshole," Perez said.

Perez was still standing inside the open doorway when Diggy, his head leaned forward in pain, said, "Ain't my fault ya mama done seen more dicks than that bitch did the World's Biggest Gangbang."

Perez stared down into the car, glowering. *"You better shut your mouth!"*

"Just shut the fuckin' door," Ballantine said, shaking his head as he climbed into the driver's seat.

Perez did as he was told, but made a point to slam the door, making Diggy and Stick snicker. Once Perez was in the passenger's seat, Stick said, "Is this the part where you drive us out into the sticks and beat the shit out of us?"

Perez turned his head so it was halfway visible to them and said, "You attacked two cops, fucko."

"They was off duty," Diggy said.

"Yeah," Stick said. "And doesn't us being ex-cops count for something?"

Ballantine chuckled. "Not to me."

"Not to me either," Perez said. "Besides, you were *dirty* cops. You made us all look bad."

"Who, us?" Diggy asked, feigning innocence.

"You were working for Benny Cordella," Ballantine said.

"You were spending Benny's money, same as us," Stick said. "You're hardly innocent."

"That was part of the job," Ballantine said. "Take the graft and look the other way. But you idiots were actually working for him."

"Running packages," Perez added. "Probably more."

"Speaking of packages," Diggy said, "I got one for ya mama, Perez."

Perez jerked forward and turned his head, realizing he had nowhere to go. Then he looked over at his partner, who was staring at him like he was stupid.

"Sit back and pop a Valium," Ballantine said.

"Yeah, chill your ass out," Stick said. "All this stress, you're liable to have yourself a heart attack."

"We wouldn't want that," Diggy said. "Be a damn shame if we had to sit here and watch you die."

"Shut up," Perez snapped.

"Look guys, this is fun, but we don't have to do this," Stick said. "Yes, those two morons back there were cops, but we all know this wasn't 'cause they were cops."

Ballantine, staring out at the street ahead, said, "Yeah, yeah, you're sore 'cause Keeling turned your asses in and got your badges taken away."

"You're lucky," Perez said. "It coulda gone a lot worse. It had been me, I'da made sure you got jail time too."

"Lucky for us it wasn't you then," Stick said.

"Ain't never gonna be you neither, 'cause you're a world-class fuck up," Diggy said. "Don't you know everybody in the precinct laughs at you behind your back?"

"You're both hypocrites," Stick said. "You're both on the take, and Keeling and that other stooge too. Who the fuck are you to lecture us about principles when you don't have any more than we do?"

"You got greedy," Ballantine said, staring at Stick in the rearview.

"Ya mama's greedy," Diggy said. "Greedy for that dick."

Before Ballantine could react, Stick looked over at Diggy. "No, no, you got it wrong, Diggy. It's *Perez's* mama who's the whore."

"Shit," Diggy said. "Both them bitches hoes."

"Just keep talkin', smartass," Perez said.

"So you are gonna take us out somewhere and beat the hell out of us," Stick said.

"Nah," Ballantine said. "You get the VIP treatment, on account of how you're former cops and all."

Perez craned his neck around to look Stick in the eyes. "There's a thing we didn't talk about."

"Oh yeah?" Stick said. "What's that?"

"We didn't talk about the real reason you don't like Keeling."

Ballantine chuckled in anticipation.

Stick glared at Perez.

Ballantine said, "Yeah, I suppose that would burn some, having a guy turn you in and get your badge taken away, and then having that same motherfucker end up banging your wife."

The two cops laughed like this was the funniest thing ever.

Ballantine looked at Stick in the rearview. "But seriously, Stick, you get Keeling pretty good tonight?"

Stick grinned a little. "I got his ass."

Diggy said, "Don't let Stick fool ya, he whupped that boy's ass!"

Ballantine chuckled. "Glad to hear it."

"What," Diggy said, "you don't like Keeling either?"

"I don't like any of you," Ballantine said. "I'd 'a been just as happy if all four of you ass clowns had killed each other."

Diggy was looking out the side window. "Where you takin' us, anyway?"

Perez chuckled.

"Don't worry about it, sweetheart," Ballantine said. "Just sit back and enjoy the ride."

CHAPTER THREE

Neither Diggy nor Stick understood what was happening when Ballantine turned the cruiser into a dark empty parking lot on Troost. They saw a black Escalade waiting. They didn't know who was in it, but they were both fairly certain it wasn't anyone they wanted to see.

There was no movement, but it was apparent that someone was inside because they could hear a pounding 808 kick drum throbbing on the stereo within. As Ballantine slowed the cruiser, sidling it up next to the SUV, Stick said, "Listen guys, we were just playing around. There's no need for anybody to get stupid here."

Perez turned his head to show Stick his profile. It was dark inside the cruiser, but Stick could still see his shit-eating grin. "Too late, Stick. You're already stupid."

Stick didn't say anything. He and Diggy just stared out the window on Diggy's side, studying the ominous Escalade. Then the passenger side door of the Escalade swung open, and Case, a heavyset Samoan who worked for Benny Cordella, stepped out, flattening down the back of his black leather jacket. Then he peered inside the cruiser at Diggy and Stick.

"Time to get out, fellas," Ballantine said. He and Perez both opened their doors and stepped out into the cool October air.

Seeing Case, Diggy and Stick relaxed. "Thank God it's you," Stick said. "For a minute there, I thought this was going to end badly."

Diggy and Stick climbed out of the cruiser, and the cops unfastened their cuffs. When they turned around, they saw that Case was now flanked by a couple of other goons.

Stick looked at Ballantine. "Thanks for the ride, fuckers." Stick expected Ballantine's smile to fall away, but it didn't. Before Stick could ponder this, Case stepped forward and delivered a hard uppercut to his midsection. Diggy considered rushing Case, but all the goons' guns came up simultaneously, all pointed at him and Stick.

"What the fuck did you do that for?" Stick asked, doubled over. "We all work for the same guy."

"Do we?" Case asked.

"What does that mean?"

"Benny wants to see you two."

Diggy stared at the unsmiling Samoan. "Is it somethin' bad?"

Case shrugged. "Depends on your perspective."

Stick straightened himself and leveled his gaze at Case. "What's your perspective?"

"You guys are through."

"What does that mean?" Diggy asked.

"Benny's not happy with you," Case said, turning toward his goons. "Load these fuckers up and let's go."

As the goons shoved Diggy and Stick into middle seats of the vibrating, hip-hop-filled Escalade at gunpoint, Perez spoke from outside. "It was real nice seeing you fellas."

He and Ballantine chuckled.

"See you never," Ballantine said, giving them a mocking wave.

"Suck my black dick, Ballantine," Diggy said.

"You boys have a nice trip," Ballantine said.

The goons closed the doors.

CHAPTER FOUR

They were driving on the dark highway. One of the goons, a heavyset Latino, sat up front, driving. Case was in the passenger seat. Diggy and Stick were in the middle row, and the other goons, one white, one black, sat behind them with their pistols aimed at the backs of their heads. There was loud music playing, some dipshit rapping about getting his dick sucked.

"Real nice music you got there," Stick said. "What do you call this?"

Case turned back to him, pointing at the stereo. "That's my cousin, Clarence."

"Makes sense," Diggy said.

Case stared at him. "What do you mean?"

Diggy looked at him through lazy, half-lidded eyes. "It means he sucks, just like you."

Case grinned, nodding. "Okay, okay." He looked back and forth at Diggy and Stick, sizing them up. "Tell you what. Let's play the 'be quiet game.' You guys ever play that when you was kids?"

"I hated that game," Stick said.

"I ain't never played it," Diggy said. "How's it work?"

Stick looked at him. "It's a bullshit game."

"But how you play?"

Case said, "You just shut the fuck up."

Diggy looked at him like he was stupid. "*That's* the game?

16

There ain't no rules?"

"Nope," Case said. "You just shut the fuck up. That's the game."

"I told you it was stupid," Stick said.

"Ain't nobody ask you," said the black goon in the backseat.

"Too bad, I said it anyway."

"You got a smartass mouth," said the white goon.

Diggy grinned and nodded. "He's right, you know. You do got a smart-ass mouth, Stick."

Stick pretended to be offended. "Who, me?"

Case's pistol came up, and it was aimed at Stick. Case was trying to look casual, like he was just resting the pistol in that position, but Stick got the point.

"You better point that gun at somebody else, Kemosabe," Stick said.

Case smiled and leaned forward like he really wanted to hear what Stick had to say. "Or what, smart guy?"

Stick winked. "You'll see."

Case chuckled with surprise. He looked over at the driver. "You hear this dude?"

The driver nodded. "I hear him."

Stick said, "I'll make you a promise, Case."

"Okay."

"If this thing goes sideways…"

Case's grin widened. "Oh, you best believe it's about to go sideways."

"Okay," Stick said, "*when* this thing goes sideways, I'm gonna kill your sorry Samoan ass."

Case laughed a hearty laugh. He looked Stick in his eyes, trying to convey seriousness. "I got news for you, Stick. You ain't gonna live that long."

"Oh yeah?" Diggy asked. "You think we gon' die?"

"You gonna die *big time*," said the black man behind them.

Diggy squinted at Case, like he was trying to understand. "When you say we gon' die, do you mean both of us, or do you

17

just mean Stick's dumb ass?"

"Both of your dumb asses," said the driver.

"I'm sorry, guys," Stick said, "but I've got a full slate this week. I'm too busy to die right now. Maybe I can pencil you in for mid-November."

Case stared at him. "You really think you're funny, don't you?"

"Hell yes, he thinks he's funny," Diggy said. "I been tryin' ta tell him for years he ain't funny, but he got a hard head, don't listen too good."

Case stared intently at Stick. "That right? You got a hard head?"

Stick grinned like he didn't have a care in the world. "It's been said."

Case winked at him. "I get the chance, I'm gonna soften that head of yours."

"What the fuck does that mean?" Diggy asked.

"That line doesn't even make sense," Stick said.

"It means I'm gonna bust a cap in it."

Diggy nodded enthusiastically, looking at Stick. "Yeah, that would probably do it." Diggy looked into Stick's eyes. "I think you need to tell 'im, Stick."

Stick looked at his partner with a bewildered expression. "Tell him what?"

Diggy narrowed his eyes. "You know."

Stick considered this for a moment.

"*Oh,*" Stick said, finally understanding. "You think I should tell him?"

"You should *definitely* tell him."

All this was making Case angry, and he finally blurted, "*What? Tell me what?*"

While Case was looking at Stick, Diggy came out of his seat with a hard right to the side of the Samoan's head. Case's head rocked back, and Stick lunged for the gun, grabbing Case's wrist. Even in his disoriented state, Case fought back and the gun moved to the right, pointing directly at the driver. The Escalade swerved and the driver turned to look at the pistol just in time to see it explode in his face, and like *that*, his brains were all over the headliner and what remained of the driver's-side window.

The black guy in the backseat raised his pistol to shoot Diggy, but the Escalade swerved hard to the left and the gunshot rang out, shooting Case in the temple, splattering his brains all over the windshield and the dash. Diggy turned toward the white goon in the back. The guy had his pistol up, but he was thrown hard into the side window. Diggy leaped over the seat and was on him in seconds. Stick was turning to help when he saw the headlights of oncoming vehicles shining in through the bloody windshield.

"*You fuckin' jig!*" the white man in the backseat screamed just before Diggy smashed his cheekbone with his fist. The guy's pistol went off, firing into the headliner. The Escalade continued veering and suddenly the entire car was filled with bright white light.

CHAPTER FIVE

When Stick opened his eyes, he was lying on a bed with a bright light pouring down at him. He blinked, turning his head away. He had no idea where he was or how he'd gotten here. He cleared his eyesight, as well as his head, which hurt like a mother-fucker, and realized he was in a hospital bed. Was he in a hospital? He looked down at his arm through squinted eyes and saw an IV and bandages. He raised his other hand and saw black bruises and more bandages. He looked to his right and saw a monitor with cords dangling from it. His eyes followed the cords to his hospital gown-covered chest, deducting they were connected to patches beneath the gown. He tried to move but felt the restraints around his waist and legs.

What the fuck?

He tried to raise his head from the pillow to look down his body but found that his neck hurt too badly for him to accomplish this.

"You finally awake, sleepyhead?" came a voice from his left. Stick looked over through slitted eyes. When he did, he saw three things. The first was his best friend, Diggy, lying unconscious in an identical bed about eight feet away. There was a blood-soaked bandage wrapped around Diggy's head. The second thing Stick saw was the heavyset white dude with a goatee and a red flannel shirt sitting in an aluminum folding chair, staring at him. The third thing he saw was the silver Mossberg pump lying across

Goatee Guy's lap.

Stick stared at him for a moment, trying to discern whether he was real or some sort of hallucination. Once he ascertained that Goatee Guy was in fact real, he asked, "Where am I?"

Goatee Guy smiled, flashing a set of pearly-white dentures. "Where do you think you are?"

Stick stared at him, too tired to be a wise ass. He tried to shake his head but wasn't sure it actually shook. "I have no idea."

"You were in a wreck on 435," Goatee Guy said. "A really nasty wreck."

When Stick heard that, it all came flooding back to him. He saw Case's pistol shoot the driver in the face. He saw the goon shoot Case. He saw the oncoming headlights swerving around them. He thought he remembered seeing Diggy launch over the seat at the guy behind them, but it was hazy.

"You guys were lucky," Goatee Guy said. "Everyone else in the truck is dead."

Stick's neck hurt, so he turned it so he was looking straight ahead. He tried to muster up the energy to continue the conversation but could not. Lucky for him, Goatee Guy went on talking without him.

"The doctors say your buddy here is gonna be okay," Goatee Guy said. "You both had concussions. This guy has some broken ribs, cracked his skull. You got a broken ankle, but that's about it."

Hearing this, Stick tried to raise his head to look down at his feet again, but found he could not. His ankle didn't hurt, so he figured he was on some sort of pain meds. That was likely what was being pumped into his arm. Simultaneously, his entire body hurt and did not hurt at all. It was unlike anything he'd ever felt. There was no single source of pain that stood out, but rather a full-body discomfort.

Stick stared ahead, focusing on the ceiling and the walls for the first time, now seeing that they were gray cement brick. He looked around the little bit he could without turning his head.

He saw that there was no TV, no clock, none of the normal hospital stuff.

He tried to turn his head toward Goatee Guy again, only managing to turn it part way.

"What you need, champ?" Goatee Guy asked.

"This...isn't a hospital," Stick said.

"Good call. Nope, not a hospital. This is a makeshift hospital room, compliments of your pal and mine, Benny Cordella. He got you guys a doctor who comes in twice a day and a nurse with a set of big tits. You'll like her. And them." He chuckled. "But the doctor...I gotta tell ya, I'm not sure about his credentials. I'm not sure he's a real doctor. At least not a people doctor."

Stick was too tired to speak. He closed his eyes and slipped off into a deep sleep.

CHAPTER SIX

Stick didn't wake up again for another two days. Even then, he only awoke when he was slapped by one of Benny's guys. Stick blinked himself awake to the sound Benny saying, "Wake his ass up." Stick opened his eyes and looked at the goon who'd slapped him, a black man with every other tooth missing. But the guy was blurry. Everything was blurry. It took Stick a moment to adjust his eyes. When he did, he saw that he was still strapped down in the bed. But this time, he found himself in a room filled with assholes. And Diggy, but then, Diggy was an asshole too.

"There he is," Benny said jovially.

Stick squinted at him but didn't say anything.

"Now that you're both awake, I got something I wanna talk to you boys about," Benny said.

Hearing this, Stick turned his head to the left—it hurt considerably less to do so now—to see Diggy lying awake in the bed next to him, looking back at him.

"You look like three hundred pounds 'a shit," Diggy said.

Stick replied, "You look like hell too."

"Well—" Diggy started, but he was cut off by Benny.

"Both you fuckers shut your mouths now."

They both looked at Benny. Benny was a heavyset bald man whom they had always joked about looking like the Kingpin in *Spiderman* comics. Except Kingpin was fat *and* muscular, whereas Benny was just fat. And not just regular fat either, but seven-thousand-calories-a-day fat. Once when Stick had been making jokes to Diggy about Benny's weight, Diggy had told him, "It ain't right to make fun of somebody's weight. That's fat-shaming, Stick." To this, Stick had responded by saying, "That rule only counts for decent folks. Benny Cordella ain't decent folks. He's one of the worst, most vile sons of mother-fuckers who ever lived. He's the kind of guy who would murder his own mama just to get the last dinner roll." While Stick had no way of knowing it, his exaggerated assessment of Benny was only the slightest bit off the mark; Benny had not murdered his mother over a dinner roll but had instead paid a crackhead to kill her when he was nineteen so he could collect her life savings, which, in the end, turned out to be a measly seven hundred ninety-four dollars.

If Benny was less than kind and more than obese, he compensated for his shortcomings with a sharpness of attire. Benny had taste, and not just for food. No one disputed that. Even if someone hated Benny, and a hell of lot of people did, they could say nothing about his exquisite clothing, which generally consisted of white suits that cost more than sports cars, topped off with a bright red silk tie and a carnation in his lapel. There were many jokes made behind Benny's back about those carnations, and some of his goons questioned how he obtained them. The truth, something that, again, no one knew, was that Helen Dorrian, an elderly florist in Westport, was into Benny for a significant chunk of change. One of the ways Helen Dorrian kept Benny happy while paying off her debt little by little was by keeping him flush in carnations.

Benny Cordella was a prick. A well-dressed prick, but a prick nonetheless. Today the prick was dressed in, you guessed it, a white suit with a red tie. He stood at the foot of Stick's bed, surrounded by his lackeys, looking back and forth from Diggy to Stick.

"See," he said, "you guys fucked me."

"Man, I musta been really drugged up, 'cause I don't remember fuckin' you at all," Diggy said. "Trust me, I've woke up to some ugly bitches, but ain't none of 'em looked like your big ass."

Stick ignored his partner's banter. "*We fucked you?*" he asked. "How you figure that?"

Benny smiled a big toothy smile that was as white as his suit. "How I figure it is, you idiots stole a haul of AR-15s in Overland Park a couple weeks back."

Stick had been groggy before, but this woke him up right quick.

"How do you know that?" Stick asked.

Benny said, "If a dog farts in an old woman's house in Olathe, I know about it before that fart is even out his ass. Anything goes on in KC, I know about it."

"Fair enough," Stick said. "But so what?"

"Yeah, so what?" Diggy said. "The dumb bastards we took 'em off of were a bunch 'a shit-kicker white supremacist dudes who live on meth and probably met their wives at their family reunions."

"So what," Benny said, grinning, letting the words hang there, "is that those shit-kicking inbreds worked for me."

"You shittin' me," Diggy said.

"No shitting involved," Benny said.

"Well hell," Diggy said, "that's a zebra of a different stripe then."

"We didn't know, Benny," Stick said. "There's no way we could have known."

"You want us to get them guns back?" Diggy asked.

Benny stared at him coldly. "Get them back? Where are they?"

"We sold them to some bikers in Chicago," Stick said.

"But we can get 'em back," Diggy said.

Benny turned and paced a few steps with his hands interlocked behind his back. "There's no need," Benny said. "There's another way you're gonna make it up to me."

"We're sorry, Benny," Stick said. "Like I said, we had no idea those guns were yours."

Benny stopped pacing and turned toward Stick, raising his finger and waggling it at him. "A good rule of thumb is, if it's in the area, I've got a hand in it. Your dumb asses shoulda known."

Neither Diggy nor Stick said a word. The truth was, he was right: they should have known.

"So you not gonna punish us then?" Diggy asked.

"You're not getting off scot-free for what you did," Benny said. "You limp dicks stole from me, and I can't allow that. But then, I shoulda known you'd steal from me. After all, you're a couple of greedy cops." He chuckled. "That's a redundant statement, huh?"

The goons who were smart enough to understand the joke chuckled. Goatee Guy was not one of them. He just stood there looking dumbfounded, trying to work it out.

"Cops are greedy by nature," Benny said.

Neither Diggy nor Stick could disagree with this assessment. They were no longer cops themselves, but neither had ever met a cop who wasn't on the take in one way or another.

"So what's the deal?" Stick asked.

Benny leveled his gaze at Stick, still grinning big. "The deal, as you say, is this...I need you two to track down a man and pay him back for something he did. A very bad thing." A pained look washed over Benny's face and he sighed heavily. "A *really* bad thing he cannot be allowed to get away with."

CHAPTER SEVEN

Diggy and Stick had been staying in the makeshift hospital for almost a week, and they were about as bored as they'd ever been. They were both awake and being babysat by Goatee Guy.

"I wish there was a TV in here," Diggy complained. "With nothin' to do but talk to your dumb ass, I'm finna lose my mind."

Stick looked over at Diggy in his bed. "Am I really that bad?"

Diggy was staring back. "Worse. Way worse."

"You two argue like an old married couple," Goatee Guy said from his chair.

Diggy shot him a scowl. "Ain't nobody ask you."

Stick was still stuck on Diggy saying he didn't like talking to him. "My teachers always said I was an excellent conversationalist."

"I dunno what to tell ya," Diggy said. "Them motherfuckers lied."

Stick looked down at his fingers, seeing a remnant of his well-chewed thumbnail sticking out close to the quick. He raised his thumb and went to work chewing at it. This was a habit he'd had since he was a young boy. It was a habit that had driven his daddy, and then, later, his first wife, Isobella, nuts. Diggy didn't care for it much either and was prone to making the occasional complaint.

"I was thinkin'," Diggy said.

Still chewing on the nail, Stick asked, "About what?"

"As boring as this is, you figure this is what it's like in prison?"

"Nah," Stick said. "There's way more to do in prison."

"Like what?"

"Lots of things," Stick said, placing his hand back on his chest. "Like, for instance, lifting weights and raping other dudes."

Diggy chuckled. "Can't say I'm much for rapin' dudes, but I suppose it would pass the time."

"Probably so," Stick said. "But, like you, I'd be happy with a television. Or maybe a book."

"You say that like you're Mr. Literature," Diggy said. "The shit you read, you'd be better off not readin' at all."

"There's nothing wrong with reading westerns."

Goatee Guy chimed in. "I read westerns all the time."

Diggy rolled his eyes. "Westerns are bullshit."

"Why's that?" Goatee Guy asked.

"Because they're racist," Diggy answered.

"Bullshit, they are," Stick said. "Westerns are *not* racist."

Diggy looked at him. "Lemme ask you somethin'. There any brothers in them books you like readin'?"

"Sometimes," Stick said. "There was a black guy—the sidekick—just a couple books back."

"How the hell would they have black people in them anyway?" asked Goatee Guy. "What would they be, slaves?"

"There was a lot of black cowboys," Diggy said. "Just 'cause you don't know about 'em don't mean they didn't exist. I don't figure you for much of a historian anyway, you goofy fucker."

"You are kind of goofy," Stick told Goatee Guy. Then he turned back to Diggy. "But yes, sometimes there are black guys in the books."

"But they sidekicks," Diggy said with disdain.

"Like you," Stick joked.

Diggy looked at him, his eyebrows raised. "That what you think, that I'm the sidekick? I got news for ya, Stick, I'm the hero. *You're* the fuckin' sidekick."

"Dwayne Figgers is nobody's sidekick."

"Whatever, man, you foolin' yourself," Diggy said. "Your ass is the sidekick."

Stick raised his hand from his chest, waving his palm at Diggy. "There are no sidekicks here. I like to think of us both as being Batman. There's no Boy Wonder here."

"Now how the hell's that gonna work? We both Batman? Batman and Batman? That shit don't make no sense, Stick."

"It sounds gay," Goatee Guy interjected.

"Okay, that's a bad example," Stick said. "Look at that movie where Batman and Superman teamed up."

"The one with Affleck?"

"Yeah."

"That movie was terrible," Diggy said.

"It was a bad movie, sure, but they still teamed up."

"Whatever," Diggy said. "You still Robin."

This banal banter continued for another half hour. It ended when the door opened and two of Benny's goons, both Hispanic, one in a suit and the other in a gray and black bowling shirt, strode in, followed by the nurse with the big tits. The goons had their pistols out. The nurse unfastened Diggy's and Stick's waists and legs, freeing them.

"Get your asses up," Bowling Shirt said. "Benny wants to see you."

CHAPTER EIGHT

Bowling Shirt and Asshole #2 led them down a long corridor with cement walls and no doors. There were hanging lights every eight or nine feet. The floor, also cement, was dusty beneath Diggy's and Stick's bare feet. Bowling Shirt led the way with the other goon behind them. The place was creepy, like an underground bunker from a World War II Nazi movie.

"Where you takin' us?" Diggy asked, his voice amplified by the corridor's acoustics.

"Just shut up and walk," said Asshole #2.

When they neared the end of the corridor, there was light pouring out onto the floor from a single open door on the right. When Bowling Shirt reached the door, he stepped back and faced them, ushering them in.

Diggy was the first one in. Stick was right behind. When they walked in, they saw Benny sitting on a wooden chair, facing them, smoking a vape pen. There were five goons sitting in wooden chairs by his sides, also facing them. One of the goons was Diggy and Stick's new pal, Goatee Guy. There were two empty wooden chairs facing Benny.

Diggy and Stick stood there for a moment, taking it all in.

"What are you waiting for?" Benny asked. "Sit your asses down."

Neither Diggy nor Stick said a word. They just sat and looked at Benny. Since they were still wearing the blue hospital gowns, their bare asses were flush against the seats.

Benny grinned. "I hope your stay here was pleasant."

"As well as can be expected, I guess," Diggy said.

"Where are we?" Stick asked.

Benny looked around at the walls admiringly. "This is my own personal bunker. If any shit goes down and I gotta disappear quick, this is where I'll go."

"You even got your own hospital down here," Diggy said.

"Not quite, but what's here comes in handy on occasion," Benny said. "We usually just use it when one of the guys gets shot up and needs medical care. Nobody's ever stayed as long as you two. But you needed to mend under my supervision."

"Are we supposed to thank you?" Stick asked dryly.

"I wasn't being altruistic," Benny said. "My motives for keeping you here and nursing you back to health were purely selfish in nature."

"Say what?" Diggy said.

"I needed you healthy enough to do the job we discussed."

Stick interlocked his fingers on his lap. "Sounds like an important job."

"Oh, it is," Benny said excitedly. "This is a really big, really important job, and I wanted it done right."

"So you want us to track down this motherfucker and beat the shit outta him?" Diggy asked.

"No," Benny said. "Not quite."

"Then what?" Stick asked.

"I want you to track him down and kill him."

Diggy and Stick both leaned forward. Stick put his palms out toward Benny. "Hey, hey," he said. "Killing people isn't our thing."

Diggy said, "We'll brawl a motherfucker all day long, but we ain't into killin' folks. Like Stick said, that ain't our bag."

"Not your bag, huh?" Benny asked, grinning. "Who the fuck are you—James Brown?"

A couple of the goons chuckled.

"You've done it before," Benny said. "What's changed?"

"We just tired of that shit," Diggy said.

"So, what are you saying?"

"We can't do it," Stick said.

"We *won't* do it," Diggy said.

Benny's gaze became hard and his smile twisted into a sneer. "You're wrong there, champ. You *will* do it. You don't have a choice."

"Every man's got a choice," Diggy said.

"If your choice is for your daughter, Alyssa, to die, Mr. Diggs, then so be it. She can die," Benny said. He turned his gaze toward Stick. "How about you, Mr. Figgers? You want your ex-wife killed?" Benny turned back to Diggy, "How about your daddy, Mr. Diggs? Would you like somebody to walk into his home on Randolph Street and stab him in the eye with an ice pick?"

"You better not touch—" Diggy began.

"Nobody's touching anybody," Benny said. "So long as you chucklefucks play ball. You do that, your loved ones get to live." Benny turned his gaze back toward Dwayne "Stick" Figgers. "You've got a kid from your first marriage. Jimmy, right? Would you like for me to have Jimmy decapitated?"

Stick's head rocked back as if he'd been punched in the face. "Jim doesn't even talk to me."

"Why's that?" Benny asked.

An expression that was equal parts guilt and embarrassment washed over Stick's features. "He sorta disowned me. He said he didn't love me anymore."

Benny grinned. "What would he think if he knew you were allowing him to be killed gruesomely...for some shit *you* did? You think that would that make him love you more, or less?"

Stick leaned forward, looking down at his folded hands.

"Who the hell is the guy you want us to go after?" Diggy asked. "We'll do it, alright? Just give us the fuckin' name and let's it get it over with."

"You don't sound too happy about it," Benny said.

"Who said we gotta be happy?" Diggy asked. "We might eat the mouthful of shit you feedin' us, but we ain't gon' be smilin' while we do it."

Benny looked at Stick, whose head was still bowed. "How about you, Mr. Figgers? You onboard?"

Stick remained slumped over for a long moment, everyone in the room's eyes on him. Then, slowly, he raised his head to look into Benny's eyes. "I'll fuckin' do it, but you're a piece of shit."

Benny chuckled. "Oh, don't I know it."

"So who's the guy?" Diggy asked.

Benny crossed his legs and raised his index finger to his chin, letting it sit there. "You boys ever hear of a guy named Dread Corbin?"

Diggy and Stick both brightened with recognition.

Stick nodded, and Diggy said, "Oh yeah, we heard of him. Everybody's heard of him. Big time smack dealer. Supposed to be mean. Sadistic. They say there's some shit wrong with his face."

"They say he looks like Freddy Krueger," Stick said.

Benny touched his fingers to his forehead and let them run down over his face. "His face is burned up," Benny said. "He doesn't quite look like Freddy Kruger, but he's not pretty."

Diggy leveled his gaze on Benny. "Dread Corbin is the guy?"

Benny nodded. "Affirmative."

"Since we're going to be the ones who kill him, can we at least ask what he did?" Stick asked.

Benny's expression changed. At first Diggy and Stick thought he looked sad, but then the sadness transformed into anger, his features hardening. "This motherfucker..." Benny stopped to compose himself. "Dread Corbin and I got into a disagreement."

"Over drugs," Stick said.

Benny shrugged. "*Business*. There was a dispute, and Dread got pissed off. Since Dread is a hothead, he wanted to get back at me."

"Dread Corbin is a bad dude," Diggy said. "What did you expect?"

Stick nodded. "I've got to agree. You lay down with dogs..."

"*I'm* a bad dude," Benny snapped.

Diggy tilted his head, smirking. "Is you, though? Is you *really?*"

Benny ignored him. "Dread wanted to get back at me, so he snatched my daughter, Emelia. Then he called me and told me he'd taken her. He let me speak to her. She was crying and..." Benny's voice cracked and his breath caught. He stopped to regain his composure. "After I spoke to her, Dread got on the phone..."

Diggy and Stick listened without speaking. They heard the pain in Benny's voice and sensed the rage behind it. "The fucker got on the line and...he said he was going to kill her. I offered him money—*lots of money*—but he wouldn't back down. Then he..." Benny paused uncomfortably. When he spoke again, there was an angry defiance in his voice. "The fucker slit her throat while I was on the line, so I could hear it."

"Jesus," Stick said.

"Jesus had nothing to do with it," Benny said.

"That's fucked up," Diggy said.

"But that ain't the half."

"There's more?" Diggy asked.

"Oh, there's more," Benny said. "Dread asked me, 'Did you know your daughter was pregnant, Benny?' I hadn't. Emelia hadn't told me. I don't know why, but...she hadn't."

Considering the man's foul demeanor and quick temper, Diggy and Stick had a pretty good idea why she hadn't told him.

"She was pregnant when he killed her?" Diggy asked.

Benny looked at them with an angry expression, nodding. *"The fucker cut the baby out of her stomach."*

"Like that actress who was married to the director," Stick said.

"That's why I'm sending you after him," Benny said.

"Seems like we'd be doin' the world a favor by killin' an evil fucker like that," Diggy said.

"There's one thing, though," Benny said. "There's a catch."

CHAPTER NINE

Diggy blinked. "There's a catch?"

Stick looked over and the two of them exchanged a look.

Benny grinned. "Silly boy, there's *always* a catch."

Diggy and Stick stared at him, waiting for what they both expected to be some bullshit. Diggy vocalized their collective concern. "This seems like this about to be some bullshit."

Benny's grin widened. Goatee Guy, sitting in the chair beside him, chuckled. Benny took a hit off his vape pen, blowing it out. "You think so, huh?"

Stick said, "Why stretch this out?"

"Yeah," Diggy said. "Just say the shit."

"Okay." Benny sat there, drawing it out, trying to make it more dramatic. "So…Dread disappeared in the wind. Nobody could find him. Even though he had a business to run, he dropped clean outta sight, let his lackeys run the biz, 'cause he knew he'd fucked up. He knew if I caught up with him, he was gonna pay, and pay *good*."

Diggy and Stick were both leaned forward, hanging on Benny's every word, waiting for the punchline.

"So we were hunting for him," Benny said. "Had a bounty on his ass."

"How much was the bounty?" Diggy asked.

"A good amount."

"I don't suppose *we're* gonna get that," Stick said.

Benny ignored this and continued. "On top of having bounty hunters from all across the country looking for him, our guys were looking too."

"Me and Russell here," Bowling Shirt said, standing a few feet to Stick's left.

Benny looked up at him, giving him the stink eye.

"So anyway," Benny said, "the motherfucker turned up the same day you morons got in the fight with those pigs in the bar." He looked at Stick. "I heard you clocked that pig Keeling good."

Stick feigned humility, shrugging. "I did all right, I guess."

"Stomped that sonofabitch is what he did," Diggy said. "And I got a couple punches in myself."

Stick looked at him like he was crazy. "I did all the work, Dig. Don't you go trying to horn in and take the credit."

"Listen, fuckhead..." Diggy began before being cut off by Benny.

"Hey," Benny said. "Pay attention."

Diggy made a point to sit erect and display exaggerated attentiveness. "I'm all ears, teach."

Benny shook his head. "Always the wise guy, huh?"

"Believe me, he's not all that wise," Stick said.

Diggy shot him a dirty look but said nothing.

"So this motherfucker Dread turns up in a motel in some middle-of-no-place shit hole in Florida," Benny said.

"So you got him then?" Stick asked, confused.

"Well," Benny said, sounding tired. "Not exactly."

"What happened?" Diggy asked.

Benny turned around and looked at Bowling Shirt. "You wanna tell him, Kenny?"

Diggy and Stick both turned to look at Bowling Shirt, who shrugged, saying, "When we got there, the motherfucker was dead."

Diggy and Stick both leaned back, tilting their heads a little. They didn't understand.

"He's dead?" Diggy asked.

"Motherfucker shot himself," said Kenny, a.k.a. Bowling Shirt.

Stick looked at him, his face twisted with puzzlement. "Let me get this straight: he shot himself and he was dead?"

Benny nodded. "Mmmm-hmmm."

"As in dead-dead?" Stick asked.

"Is there any other kind?" Benny asked.

"He could have been a zombie," Stick said dryly.

"I like to think he committed suicide to outrun my wrath," Benny said. "But I don't know. Anyone who can do the shit…the shit he did to my Emelia…motherfucker's got issues."

Diggy said, "I thought you wanted us to kill him."

Benny met his gaze. "Sort of, but not exactly."

"How the fuck you want us to sort of not exactly kill somebody?" Diggy said.

"Someone who's already dead," Stick added.

"That's the catch I mentioned," Benny said.

Benny took another hit off the vape pen, causing him to cough and sputter. Goatee Guy asked him if he needed a glass of water, but Benny shook his head, still trying to clear his throat. Finally, he got back to the conversation.

"Sorry about that," Benny said.

"So, how the fuck you want us to kill a dude that's already dead?" Diggy said.

"Are you guys Christians?"

"I'm a Baptist, born and raised," Diggy said. He turned to look at Stick. "But not this motherfucker. He's a godless heathen."

"I prefer atheist," Stick said.

"God ain't gonna care what the fuck you call it," Diggy said.

Before this could go any further, Benny said, "I'm a Christian. Been a Christian my whole life."

"It shows," Diggy said sarcastically. "The way you kill folks and sell drugs and all that, yeah, it definitely shows that you're a man of God."

"The Bible says a man goes to Hell when he commits suicide,"

Benny said. "Do you believe that?"

Diggy nodded. "Of course I do."

"It's the unforgivable sin," Benny said. "So, by that logic, we know Dread Corbin is in hell."

"Maybe God's not a Christian," Stick said. "Have you ever considered that? But even more important, what the fuck can we do about Dread Corbin now?"

Benny grinned. "You two are gonna go to Hell and track him down. Get revenge on his ass and avenge my Emelia. Let him know that nobody fucks with Benny Cordella."

"*Go to hell?*" Diggy said. "Now, how in tha fuck we gon' do *that?*"

Benny sat there grinning. He raised his index finger to his temple like a gun and pretended to shoot himself. "You're going to kill yourselves."

CHAPTER TEN

"What the fuck are you talking about, Benny?" Stick asked.

Diggy glared at the man. "Either you're on drugs or you got one sick sense of humor."

Benny sat back in his chair and held his hands out to the side like a grand showman. "Who's joking, Mr. Diggs? I assure you I'm not."

Maybe it was the look in Benny's eyes, maybe it was the tone of his voice, but Diggy and Stick realized at that moment that they were caught up in some crazy shit they couldn't get out of. *Dangerous* crazy shit.

They sat there in shock, staring at the smiling crime lord with their mouths hanging open. The tension in the air was as thick as a steel beam. Stick tried to speak but struggled to find the words. Before he could locate them, Diggy sprang out of his chair with his arms outstretched toward Benny. Before he could reach the man, one of the goons—a muscular Hispanic—clocked Diggy in the side of the head with his Sig Sauer. The pistol striking Diggy's skull made a loud *thwack* sound, and Diggy dropped to the floor like a bag of bricks.

Stick sat forward, staring at his wounded partner lying on the floor. Stick looked at the goons, who were all on their feet or pushing themselves up, all with their guns out. Only Benny and Stick remained seated.

"You're a fucking crazy person," Stick said.

"Maybe, maybe not," Benny said. "Either way, you cock-suckers are going."

Stick's eyes were filled with fire and anger. "To hell."

"Yes, Mr. Figgers, to hell."

"What if there is no hell?"

Benny's expression didn't change. "Then you won't even know you're gone." Benny stared into Stick's eyes. "You're an atheist. Let me ask you, which alternative is better in your opinion—hell or nothingness?"

Stick glared at him and then spat in his direction, the spittle reaching Benny's leg. Stick couldn't say which would be better or worse. Both options were shit.

Diggy was starting to stir, and all the goons' pistols raised in his direction.

"Please don't do this," Stick said, his voice filled with desperation.

Benny held his open palms out to his sides. "I've got no choice."

Stick's eyes welled up with tears. "You're a maniac."

Diggy was trying to raise himself to his feet now but was having difficulty. Benny looked at him. "Russell, help Mr. Diggs get up." Russell hesitated for a moment, and it was evident he was afraid of Diggy. Nevertheless, he slid his Glock into his waistband and went to Diggy, crouching down to pull him up. Diggy didn't fight him, and Russell hefted him up. Once he was back on his feet, he swiveled and set Diggy back down in his chair.

Stick looked over at his best friend, who now looked bloody, dazed, and confused. "You okay, Dig?"

Diggy looked at him wearily, as if he was struggling to hold his head up. "Nah, man," he panted. "And you ain't either."

Stick looked into Benny's eyes. "What if we don't do what you say?"

"You already know" said Goatee Guy, standing now.

Benny nodded. "You do. Your ex-wife and your son die

40

gruesome deaths. Deaths so gruesome they'd make Jeffrey Dahmer puke."

Stick just stared at him, trying to find a way out, but he saw none.

Benny looked at Diggy. "And Mr. Diggs's daddy gets an ice pick in his eye. But that's just for starters. I won't let my guys jam it all the way in, killing him. No, they'll just pluck the old fucker's eyes out. Then they'll cut pieces off the man, one by one. Maybe torture him with fire, shit like that. And his daughter, Alyssa…We'll all take turns raping her before we even start her torture."

Barely able to hold his head up, Diggy looked at him. "Let's get this shit over with, you talky bitch."

"Whoa, whoa," Stick said. "We've gotta talk this shit out."

Diggy looked at him. "What's there to talk about?"

"I don't know about you," Stick said, "but I'm not in a hurry to die."

Staring into Stick's eyes, Diggy said, "You see any other way?"

"No," Benny answered for him. "There isn't any other way. You gotta kill yourselves, then you gotta go after Dread Corbin."

An exhausted Stick stared at Benny and repeated, "In hell."

Benny nodded. "Yep."

"Okay, so…" Diggy began with some effort, "if your plan works and we go to Hell, how's this supposed to work?"

Benny looked confused. "You go after Dread."

"I get that part, fuckhead, but what do we do when we catch him? He's already dead, so what can we possibly do to him?"

Benny crossed his arms. "To be honest, I'm not sure, Mr. Diggs, I guess we'll see."

"This shit don't make no sense."

"Fuck no," Stick said. "This plan is as stupid as you and your goons are, Benny."

"Stupid or not, you're going," Benny said.

CHAPTER ELEVEN

Diggy and Stick were on their knees, right beside each other with guns to their heads. They were surrounded by Benny's goons, and they all had their guns out. Benny was somewhere behind them, so they couldn't shoot him when they were given pistols.

Diggy looked up at the big Hispanic man looming over him. "Is it really necessary for us to be down here on our knees? This fuckin' floor hurts."

"Shut your cockhole," Herman said from their left.

Stick was still trying to talk his way out of it.

"Come on, Benny, be reasonable," Stick said, trying to hide his fear. "One, we don't even know for a fact Hell exists—"

"Of course we do," Benny's voice said from behind. "There's proof."

"Bullshit," Stick said. "There's absolutely no proof that any of that hoodoo shit is real."

Diggy spoke up. "I'm a Christian man, Benny, you know that. But there ain't no goddamn proof of no Hell. You just makin' shit up now just to hear yourself speak."

"Two," Stick continued, "even if there is a Hell, and even if we get there, Dread Corbin is already dead and in Hell. It's doubtful that we could even do anything to hurt him. Because how can you hurt someone who's already dead and in the afterlife?"

"Stick is right," Diggy said. "How the fuck we gon' hurt a

42

man who's already dead and in Hell? That shit don't make sense, Benny."

There was a long pause indicating Benny might be considering this. Then he said, "Either way, you two are going. End of story."

"Can I say one thing?" Diggy asked.

"One thing, Mr. Diggs."

"Fuck you."

"Fuck me?"

"Yeah," Diggy said, nodding. "And fuck your mother. That's all I got to say."

"Hand them your pistols." Diggy and Stick weren't sure who Benny was speaking to, but then the goons standing in front of them held out their pistols. As they did this, Benny reminded them, "You try any slick shit, and I'll make sure all your loved ones die. You'll die today, they'll die tomorrow."

Diggy and Stick took the pistols begrudgingly. They were on their knees, staring down at the guns.

Diggy turned halfway around, but he still couldn't see Benny. "You want us to shoot ourselves?"

"Yes," Benny said. "You're gonna die either way, but you don't have to take the people you love with you. And…this is important. When you get to Hell, you'd better hold up your end—"

"Killin' ourselves ain't enough to hold our end?" Diggy asked.

"Not by a long shot," Benny said. "You go there and you take care of this fuck."

Stick felt like he was going to hyperventilate. He wanted to ask Benny how he would even know whether or not they went after Dread Corbin if they went to Hell, but he couldn't seem to make himself speak. Diggy, however, had no such problem. "How you even gonna know if we go after that fucker or not?"

"I'll get a medium. Somebody who talks to dead people like that *Sixth Sense* kid. And if I find out you didn't do your part, then guess what?"

"What?"

"Your loved ones go down for the dirt nap."

"Man, this some bullshit," Diggy said.

The stress and anxiety of the situation was too much for Stick, and his stomach gave way and he vomited all over the Hispanic guy's bright white Puma sneakers. The goon jumped back and screamed, *"Jesus Christ!"* just before Stick got sick again, this time on the floor.

"Look what you did to my sneakers, maricón!" the goon yelled, kicking Stick hard in the stomach. Stick's stomach already hurt, and the pain from the kick did nothing to help. Stick's body flopped back, putting pressure on his left ankle, causing pain to shoot through it.

Diggy was staring directly at the Hispanic cat when Benny's bullet hit the fucker in his eye. At the same time he heard the shot, Diggy saw the goon's brains fly out the back of his head before he toppled onto the floor.

There was a silence, everyone trying to make sense of the situation.

"I'm...sorry about that," Benny said, sounding sincere. "Anyway, shooting yourselves in the head is gonna be a bitch, no two ways about it. I think it might be easier if you counted down together so you fire at the exact same moment. If you don't, it's gonna be harder for the guy who pulls the trigger last. But it's on you. You do it however you like."

Stick's stomach hurt and he felt like he could vomit again at any second. Diggy could feel his heartbeat in his throat. There were tears in Stick's eyes when he gasped, "Please, Benny." Diggy looked over at his partner. "Stay strong, man. Fuck these motherfuckers. Don't let 'em see you cry. Just do the damn thing and get it over quick. Go out with dignity. Go out strong, Stick. They gon' kill us either way, so fuck 'em."

"Put the pistols in your mouths," Benny said.

Stick took a deep breath. He and Diggy stuck the Glock

barrels into their mouths.

Stick felt hot, like he might pass out. Despite Diggy's encouragement, he could feel tears welling up in his eyes. He didn't want to die, not like this, surrounded by fuckheads. But he knew this was how it had to be. There was no way out.

Stick said "fuck," but the pistol in his mouth made the word unintelligible. The barrel and its metal taste gagged him, so he tried to take deep breaths around it.

"Start the countdown," Benny said. There was a long pause and no one spoke. "Oh shit, I'm sorry, I forgot," Benny said. "You've got pistols in your mouths and can't talk. Let me count down for you."

Diggy and Stick had the same thought; hopefully Benny counted down from ten, buying them a few extra seconds. Both men were more frightened than they had imagined possible. Both men also weighed the pros and cons of pulling the pistols out from their mouths and shooting the goons. There was no way they could shoot them all, and such an action would be the same as signing death warrants for their families.

"You find that fucker Corbin and you make him pay," Benny said. "And you tell him who sent you."

Diggy felt warm tears cascading down his face. He wanted to look over to see if Stick was crying too, but he didn't. *Couldn't.* But Stick *was* crying.

"Three," Benny said, starting the countdown.

The reality of the situation became ever more apparent. Their fingers tensed on the triggers. Their minds raced, searching for a solution to a problem with no solutions.

"Two."

Diggy's and Stick's eyes were closed. Diggy was picturing his daughter in his mind. The words "please God" popped into his head. Next to him, Stick was thinking about time when he and Tina had been happy. In his mind's eye, she was smiling at him, mouthing the words "I love you."

Their fingers tightened a little more on the triggers. Neither of them had any desire to remain alive to witness the other's suicide.

"*One.*"

Diggy and Stick squeezed their triggers.

CHAPTER TWELVE

Diggy opened his eyes and blinked to adjust them. He was lying on a bed, staring up at white ceiling panels. He was confused. He felt like he'd just awakened from a terrible dream. Where was he?

"Robert Diggs, number 876-B-394201-Q," said a man's voice from his left.

Diggy craned his neck toward the voice to see who it belonged to. When he did, he saw a bespectacled bald man in a white jacket who looked like he might be a doctor, looking down at a clipboard. There was a brown-haired man standing beside him, staring down at a clipboard of his own.

Diggy looked around, seeing an impossible number of beds with men in them on both his right and left. The walls were white. The ceiling was white. The floors were white. *Everything* was white.

"Where the hell am I?" Diggy asked.

The bald man looked up at him, giving him the kind of expression you'd give an idiot. "You're in a way station, Mr. Diggs."

"Way station number 983-Q9BGR to be exact," said the brown-haired man.

Diggy sat up and spun his legs around, throwing them over the side of the bed.

"Way station?" Diggy asked, trying to understand.

Then he remembered. Benny and the goons. The guns. Stick.

"This might sound like a dumb question, but...*am I dead?*"

The two men looked at him incredulously and snickered.

"I'm only going to hear that question about a thousand more times today," remarked the bald man.

The brown-haired man met Diggy's gaze and grinned. "Dead as Caesar."

"I don't know Caesar," Diggy said. "Is he dead?"

"Oh yes, he's definitely dead."

Sitting on the bed with his feet hanging off, Diggy pressed his palm against his forehead, trying to make sense of this. Then he looked up. "Okay, where's my man Stick?"

The bald man squinted. *"Stick?"*

"Dwayne Figgers," Diggy said. "They call him Stick on account of it soundin' like 'stick figure.'"

They stared at him.

Diggy shrugged. "Yeah, I know, it's a stupid fuckin' nickname. I ain't give it to him. But Stick was with me when I died. He's dead too." He paused. "At least I think he is. His ass better be dead, 'cause I ain't goin' through all this shit by myself."

The bald man stared at him with a blank expression. "I don't know what to tell you. I'm just an orderly."

Diggy looked down the row of beds, looking to see if any of the men sitting on, lying on, or standing beside them, was Stick. None of them was. Diggy stood, realizing he was wearing his red and black Jordans. He knew he hadn't been wearing sneakers when he died, so this confused him even more. He turned to scan the beds behind him, but there was no Stick to be found there either.

The two orderlies were going on to the next bed when Diggy said, "If Stick and I died together, would he be here too? Or could he be someplace else?"

The brown-haired orderly shrugged. "He could be anywhere."

Diggy furrowed his brow. "What you mean *anywhere?*"

"At any of the way stations."

"How many way stations are there?"

"Thousands," the bald man said.

The two orderlies moved on, no longer interested in Diggy.

He sat back down on the edge of the bed. The man in the bed in front of him was an elderly white man who was sound asleep. Diggy's eyes moved ahead to the next bed, where he saw the back of a sleeping man's head.

What had he gotten himself into?

CHAPTER THIRTEEN

After Diggy had waited for what he guessed was about half an hour, a twenty-something black orderly escorted him and a handful of other men down a labyrinth of halls to a gigantic auditorium that looked like the inside of an airport. But there were no bars, newsstands, or restaurants—just a huge room filled with thousands of seats, almost all filled, everyone sitting as if they were waiting for their planes. But there were no windows, only white walls, and Diggy seriously doubted there were any planes.

"What the hell is this place?" Diggy asked.

The very busy, very preoccupied orderly said, "This is where everybody gets sorted out."

"*Sorted out?*" asked a confused elderly white man standing beside Diggy.

"To find out where you're supposed to go from here."

"As in Heaven or Hell?" asked Diggy.

The orderly gave a half-hearted nod. "Something like that. 'Cept they don't call them that. Everything in the afterlife is different than you were told back on Earth."

"How so?" asked a middle-aged white man wearing a black leather jacket over a Celtics T-shirt.

"I don't have time to explain it to you, and that ain't my job," explained the orderly. He nodded out toward the rows of seats. "All of you go and find yourselves a seat."

"Then what?" Diggy asked.

"Someone will come for you."

"How they gon' find us?"

"I assure you they will."

"How long—"

"Just sit down and wait," snapped the orderly. Then he turned and headed back in the direction they'd come from.

Diggy and the other men looked at one another, a couple of them shrugging.

"Well, ain't this a bitch?" Diggy said.

The elderly white man nodded. "It does in fact appear to be a bitch."

CHAPTER FOURTEEN

Diggy didn't have to wait long. It wasn't more than ten or fifteen minutes by his estimation. As he'd sat he'd noticed some things that had piqued his interest. The first had seemed ridiculously obvious once he'd noticed it: there were no women in the room. There were thousands of men, but not a single woman. This caused him to wonder where they were. Probably a different part of the way station. Second, he noted that there were men of all different ages. If they were dead, why were they all different ages? He wondered if they would forever remain the age they'd been when they'd died. Or maybe, he thought, once a person left the way station, their appearance—their age, color, height, weight, ethnicity—transformed into something different. Maybe they'd look like angels or demons or some shit like that. Looking around, Diggy saw men of varying ethnicities—Asian, Middle Eastern, etc. No one was talking, so he couldn't be sure they spoke different languages, but it seemed likely. This led to the inevitable questions of whether or not there would be other languages spoken in the places they were going.

In the brief time he sat waiting, Diggy looked around at the other men and tried to guess where each one was going. This game proved to be more difficult than he'd anticipated. Studying the faces of the men around him, Diggy wasn't able to glean many details about them or the lives they'd led on Earth. The game was soon interrupted by a twenty-something Asian orderly who walked right up to him, stopped, and said, "Bobby Diggs, come with me."

As Diggy raised himself up from the chair, he asked, "Where we goin'?"

"It's time for your judgment."

CHAPTER FIFTEEN

Diggy had a pretty good idea how his judgment was gonna go. When Diggy was a young man, his mama always said he'd been born bad. Diggy didn't really believe that, but looking back on his life now, he could see he'd done everything in his power to perpetuate her claim.

When he was a young boy, he had done all the normal bad boy things like stealing, fighting, lying, and cussing. There had been a gang of tough boys at his elementary school who liked to pick on the smaller boys. Diggy mostly kept to himself, so they saw him as a target. But those bullies quickly learned the error of their ways. There had been five or six of the little fuckers, and they'd caught him walking down an alley on his way home from school.

Diggy was ten, a full year older than them since he'd been held back for fucking off and not doing schoolwork, so it might have been tempting to believe that was how he was able to beat those boys to a bloody pulp. But then again, there had been a gang of them and only one Diggy. Nevertheless, Diggy left them all lying bloodied on the pavement with swollen lips, cheeks, and eyes. It had been a fair fight—as fair as a five-or-six-on-one fight could be—and Diggy hadn't had to grab a pipe or a bottle to whip them. He'd done it fair and square, all on his own. But, if things had gone differently and Diggy had needed to pick up an object to overcome them, he would have. But Diggy was a natural-born scrapper, and he, as his daddy was prone to say, whipped the black off those boys' asses. After that, they never bothered him again.

Diggy lost his virginity when he was twelve. That was a fairly normal age for a boy in his neighborhood to lose his virginity, but Diggy accomplished this coming-of-age milestone in a different way than most others: he lost his to Mrs. Diaz, his caramel-complected home room teacher. Had people known, a lot of them would have asserted that Mrs. Diaz was depraved or perverted or a child molester or whatever else, but Diggy had never seen it that way. In his eyes, even then at that young age, he had been a man, and Mrs. Diaz had simply recognized that. And while it's pretty much impossible for a twelve-year-old virgin boy to properly please an adult woman, Diggy had gone through life certain he'd done just that.

That had been a significant year for Diggy, because that was also the year he went to juvie for the first time. Diggy was leaving his cousin Ray's apartment in the Wayne Minor Projects around eleven one night. He'd just climbed on his black-and-yellow Huffy bike and was about to head home when he was stopped by an older boy with a butterfly knife and ambitions of stealing his bike. A fight ensued, and in the end, the boy did not take Diggy's bike—a bike Diggy himself had stolen. Instead, the boy got nine stitches in his face, and Diggy got a six-month vacation in the Jackson County Juvenile Detention Center.

When Diggy was released, it only took him three months to run afoul with the law again. This time, at thirteen, he stole a car and took it joyriding. But the car he stole was a police cruiser. That little adventure got him sent back to Jackson County. After that, Diggy vowed he would never go back to jail, and he never did.

This isn't to imply he'd corrected his behavior, though. To the contrary, young Diggy became wilder and wilder and more out of control. He went to work slinging crack with his cousin, Harold. The two of them made a lot of money, and Diggy dropped out of high school. He and Harold then expanded their operations and started running girls. By the time he turned sixteen, Diggy had shot two men. Both of them had lived, and he got away with both shootings. When Diggy was seventeen, he killed a man for the first time. It wasn't something he was proud of, nor was it something he had aspired to do. The man he'd killed had raped his girlfriend, Kenya. She had been sixteen and the rapist had been forty-one. The man was a heroin addict with a long rap sheet, so no one even bothered searching for his killer, and once again, Diggy got away scot-free.

Harold was killed in a drive-by when Diggy was eighteen. After Diggy had gone and found the guy who'd pulled the trigger—Diggy's second murder, if you're keeping score—his daddy sat him down and convinced him to go straight.

"Those streets out there'll kill you just as sure as a bullet," his daddy had said. "You're a young man. If you go back and get your GED, you can make somethin' of yourself. You can get your narrow ass up out these streets. It ain't too late, Diggy. But if you keep fuckin' 'round out there, you mark my words, those streets are gonna get your ass." His daddy had looked at him with tears in his eyes. "Since your mama passed on, God rest her soul, you're all I got left in this world, and I don't wanna see you get caught up in all this triflin'-ass bullshit and get gunned down in the street like a damn dog."

Diggy couldn't say what exactly it was about his daddy's words that had affected him, but the words sank in and Diggy changed his life. At least somewhat. After passing his GED, Diggy's cousin Ray convinced him to join the police force and become a cop like him. But Ray's selling points weren't what Diggy's daddy would have hoped they'd be.

"Bein' a cop is like a license to steal," Ray had explained. "Shit, I do more hustlin' now than I did when I was in the streets. 'Cept now I do it legal. Now I get paid by the city, which means I don't get into trouble doin' the shit, and then I get paid takin' the graft and doin' all kinds of other shit. Can I tell you a secret, cuz?" Ray had leaned in close despite their being the only two people in the room. "I make more money bein' a cop than I ever made selling product."

That was all it took. Those were the words that sent Bobby Diggs down the path to becoming a cop.

CHAPTER SIXTEEN

In a different way station far away from the one Diggy was in, Stick was being led toward his own judgment and contemplating the many wicked deeds he'd done in his own life.

CHAPTER SEVENTEEN

Stick was born in a backwater Oklahoma town that boasted sixty-seven residents, one stoplight, no gas station, and a rickety old Baptist church that served as the meetup spot for area Klansmen. Stick's daddy, Gary Figgers, was one of those self-proclaimed good ol' boys. This was just one of the many reasons Stick had never felt even the slightest bit bad about putting a dent in his old man's head with a baseball bat when he was eleven. When Stick had walloped his daddy, Gary Figgers had been beating the ever-loving shit out of Stick's mama. Stick hadn't known much at that age, but he'd known without a doubt that there was something very wrong with his daddy straddling his mama on the floor and pounding on her face with both fists. When Stick's Louisville Slugger connected with his daddy's head, it made a solid *thwack* sound like George Brett connecting with a hanging curveball. On the third wallop, Stick had seen his mama's bloodied face staring at him with big round eyes and her mouth hanging open. "You'd better stop, Dwayne, baby," she'd whispered. "If you kill his ass, we're both gonna have some answering to do." So Stick had stopped pounding Daddy's head in, and the official story Mama came up with was that Daddy had an accident working in the field. Something having to do with his combine. No one ever investigated the matter any further, because no one gave two shits about Gary Figgers. After that, Daddy took up permanent residency at the Norman

State Hospital.

Mama tried her damnedest to raise Stick for a piece, but the following summer, she fell in love with the very married town minister and ran off somewhere, never to be seen again. At least not by Stick. As a result of her leaving, Stick was shipped off to live with his cousins in Tulsa. His uncle's name was Dick, and his cousin's name was Dick, too, so they were known as Big Dick and Little Dick. Stick liked them just fine, but mostly he liked Little Dick's sister, Carlita. He liked her so much that he screwed her out back in the tool shed. Of course, he wound up falling in love with her as young boys who'd just lost their virginity were wont to do. So when Carlita told him she'd already been deflowered by her daddy, Big Dick, when she was six, Stick believed it his duty to avenge her purity. In thirteen-year-old Stick's mind, the proper way to do this was to set Big Dick on fire while he slept in his bed. His morbidly obese uncle went up in a ball of flames, just as Stick had planned, but the fire had then gotten out of hand and also killed Little Dick and Stick's beloved Carlita. No one suspected Stick of committing the crime, so he was sent to foster care, being passed around from one house to another.

When Stick was eighteen, he enlisted in the Army. He didn't do it out of patriotism so much as he was bored and without direction. After basic training and advanced individual training at Fort Leonard Wood, Stick was stationed at Fort Lee, Virginia, where he worked in supply. By the time Stick was twenty-one, he'd attained the rank of sergeant. During this time, Stick's life was relatively calm beyond his stealing and selling military supplies off base. However, his military career came to an abrupt end when he socked a three-star general after said general caught him doing the tube steak boogie with his wife.

After that, Stick bounced around from place to place and job to job, finally landing in Kansas City, Missouri. It was then he'd gotten the wild hair up his ass and came up with the ridiculous idea to join the police department.

After two years on the job, Stick was assigned a new partner—a smartass black guy named Bobby Diggs. "But you can call me Diggy," he'd said. Stick had then held out his hand for him to shake, telling him, "And you can call me Stick." The two men soon became friends, eventually becoming tighter than a virgin's asshole on prom night. They were thick as thieves, you might say. And that would have been apt since Diggy and Stick *were* thieves.

CHAPTER EIGHTEEN

The orderly led Diggy to another corridor, and Diggy was struck by how similar it felt to walking alongside Stick toward the room where they'd died. The walls were white, and there was no sound except for the quiet squeak of Diggy's sneakers. It wasn't his style to keep quiet, but this was a whole new ballgame. This was the afterlife, and Diggy didn't have a clue what the hell—*pun intended*—he was in for.

They came to a dark blue door at the end of the corridor. The orderly knocked gingerly on it, and a man's voice told them to enter. The Asian orderly opened the door, pulling it outward, ushering Diggy in. Diggy entered the room, which was different. Inside this room, everything was baby blue.

Diggy stood in the doorway, taking in his surroundings. "You some color-coordinatin' motherfuckers, ain't ya?"

There was a very serious-looking (read: stick up his ass) older white man sitting behind a desk, facing him. "Have a seat, Mr. Diggs."

There was only one chair and it faced the man. Diggy sat, staring at him. As he did, he made the connection that the guy looked like Peter Cushing.

"Anybody ever tell you you look like that dude from *Star Wars*?"

The stick-up-his-ass serious man's mouth moved a little, and Diggy guessed that was as close as he ever came to smiling.

"I'm going to be your judge today, Mr. Diggs," the man said. "This will be a quick process."

Diggy was still looking around, despite there being nothing else in the room except for the two men, a desk, and the chairs they sat in. Diggy thought maybe it was the emptiness of the room that startled him, like he expected to notice that there was in fact something else—some other table or bookcase—hidden away in one of the corners. But there was not. There was only baby blue nothingness.

"The reason you are here is to determine, based on the deeds in your life, whether you are worthy to continue on to Nirvana—"

"*Nirvana?*"

"It's the better of the two destinations."

"Don't you already know where I'm goin'?" Diggy said. "I mean, I committed suicide."

The man sighed. "Nothing about death is what Earth people believe it to be. Suicide is not enough to exclude a person from Nirvana."

"Oh good," Diggy said, relaxing some. "Then maybe I'm good enough."

The judge gave him a stern look. "Okay..." He let the words hang there for a moment before continuing. "We will look at clips of twelve significant events from your life," he said. "From those clips, I will make the decision."

Diggy looked at him deathly serious now. "So, if I don't go to Nirvana..."

The man smiled. Holy shit, an actual fucking smile.

"*Hell?*" Diggy asked.

"*Hades*, Mr. Diggs, Hades. But the concept is the same."

Diggy shook his head, looking down, trying to wrap his head around this.

"Are we ready to begin?" the judge asked.

Diggy just stared at him.

"Clip one," announced the judge. As he said the words, an image appeared on the wall behind him. The man did not turn to look at it. He watched Diggy's expression. The clip showed a sixteen-year-old Diggy sunk down in a couch in his then-girlfriend Kenya's apartment. Kenya was snuggled up beside him, and the two of them were staring into one another's eyes. They kissed, and sixteen-year-old Diggy said "I love you" to a girl for the first time.

"You displayed genuine affection for Kenya," the judge said.

Diggy looked at him and grinned. "That's good, right?"

The judge's expression remained flat. "Keep watching."

The scene skipped ahead. Kenya stood to go to the bathroom.

"This was eighteen minutes later," the judge said.

Diggy watched his younger self staring at an orange pill bottle setting on the coffee table. He looked in the direction where Kenya had gone. Seeing that the coast was clear, he stuck the pill bottle into his pocket.

The clip froze.

"Kenya's mother had had a heart transplant, isn't that right, Mr. Diggs?"

Diggy just stared at him.

"That was her anti-rejection medicine, the medicine she needed to stay alive, and yet you stole it."

"She didn't die, though," Diggy said. "She lived a lotta years after that."

"Why did you take the pills?"

Wearing a guilty expression, Diggy shrugged. "I thought maybe they would get me high."

Neither the position of the judge's head nor his expression changed. "And did it, Mr. Diggs? Did it make you high?"

Diggy slumped in his seat. "No."

"Let's look at clip number two."

The second clip appeared on the wall. This one showed a fifteen-year-old Diggy sitting on a porch smoking a blunt with a kid from the block who called himself Cash Money. Cash Money had dreads and wore a blue KU jacket. He was staring at Diggy.

"I know it was you that stole that money outta the cabinet," Cash Money said. "That was my grandma's money. She saved that money for a long, long time. It's all she had."

Diggy turned toward him, smirking nonchalantly. "I don't know what you talkin' about. I ain't steal shit, man."

Cash Money looked at him gravely. "Please, Diggy, *please*, just give me the money back. I don't even care that you took it. I promise I'll never say another word about it, *ever*, but my grandma needs that money back."

As the clip continued, teenage Diggy became enraged. There was some screaming, and the clip concluded with Diggy shooting Cash Money in the stomach and stalking away.

The judge stared at him with a flat expression. "What do you have to say about this incident?"

Diggy sat forward and opened his palms toward the judge. "He ain't die, though. Neither of 'em died, so who cares?"

"Why did you shoot him?"

Diggy became defensive and his eyes flashed anger. "He was accusin' me of stealin' his grandma's money. I didn't appreciate that. It pissed me off."

"But you *did* take the money."

"I did," Diggy said, his lips pursed. "But that ain't the point."

"Let's look at clip number three."

And the clip began.

CHAPTER NINETEEN

Stick was sitting in an identical room in a different way station watching twelve events from his own life play out. His judge was a short Kenyan man, and like Diggy's judge, his eyes remained locked on Stick.

"Clip eight," said the judge.

The clip played, showing a thirteen-year-old Stick standing outside in darkness. He was grinning a joyful grin, and the older, deader version of Stick wondered what the hell the young boy was looking at. He saw that the unseen light source which lit his face was flickering.

And Stick knew.

"Do you know what's happening in this scene, Mr. Figgers?"

"No," Stick lied.

"You do, but I will say it anyway," the judge said. "This is you watching your uncle's house burn down with your uncle and your cousins inside." The judge stared at Stick and the two of them made eye contact. "Do you see the delight in your eyes?"

"Turn it off."

"You loved Carlita, and yet you took delight in her death. Why is that?"

Stick stared at him, saying nothing. Not because he didn't want to, but because he wasn't sure of the answer himself.

"Clip nine," said the judge.

The clip showed Stick, age ten, playing with some friends.

They were behind old man Duggars's shack, huddled around a scrawny classmate named Sherman Petrie. Everyone was giggling maniacally. Everyone except Sherman, who had a rope tied around his neck and was being hoisted off the ground. Sherman dangled for a brief moment, his eyes bulging and his face turning purple. The boys on the ground were giggling harder than ever now. Sherman's feet were kicking and he was on the verge of death when the tree branch broke and dropped him to the ground.

The clip showed a close-up of Stick's clearly disappointed face.

The judge stared at him. "Why did you try to hang Sherman?"

"We were playing Nuremberg," Stick explained. "We were Nazi hunters and Sherman was the Nazi."

"So you were hanging him."

"We were hanging him, but it was just a game. We didn't know…"

"But you *did* know, Mr. Figgers. You absolutely did know, didn't you? You were fully aware of what would have happened if that branch hadn't snapped, and you were fine with it."

"I was just one of several kids playing a game."

"Do you remember whose idea it was to play that game?"

"I don't recall."

The judge tilted his head, staring at him. "Shall I rewind the clip so we can find out?"

Stick sighed. "Okay, I get it. I was a bad kid. But I was just a kid. And surely it's gotta count for something that we didn't actually kill him."

The judge shot him a nasty look. "Oh, you're right, Mr. Figgers, you didn't kill anybody in *this* incident." He paused. "Next clip. This is a clip of you and your partner, Mr. Diggs, a week before your death."

The clip came to life. It was Diggy and Stick in the toy store, giving money to little Tiffany.

Stick sat forward and said, "Finally, a good deed."

"Just a couple of Good Samaritans, huh?"

"Yes, sir."

"And why, Mr. Figgers, did you two feel the need to take care of Tiffany?"

"Her daddy was a drug dealer who got himself killed. We wanted to help her so she wouldn't go without. We routinely sent her mother envelopes of cash with a note telling her the money was for the kid."

The judge raised an eyebrow. "Who killed Tiffany's father?"

"He was killed by Benny Cordella."

"Why?"

"He made a deal with the feds and was going to testify against him. That would have sent Benny away for the rest of his life."

The judge stared at him. "Tiffany's daddy was in police custody, was he not?"

Hearing this, the truth dawned on Stick. He looked up at the judge. "He was."

"How did Benny's men locate him?"

Stick just stared at him.

"Isn't it true that Mr. Diggs and yourself were only helping that kid because you felt guilty for telling Benny where her father was hiding, and thus basically killing him yourself?"

Stick sighed and looked down at the floor. He considered this. He looked up at the judge. "But we didn't kill the guy. Maybe...*maybe* we were inadvertently responsible, but..."

"You were directly responsible," the judge said, glaring at him. "Two cops were killed in that attack."

"We didn't pull the trigger."

"But you *had* pulled the trigger for Benny Cordella before."

A clip came on showing Diggy and Stick sitting on metal bleachers. The same clip played during both men's hearings at almost the same time.

CHAPTER TWENTY

Diggy and Stick were on the bleachers in front of an empty little league baseball field. Benny sat between them. Benny's muscle, Case, the big Samoan, was sitting two rows down with his body twisted to face them. It was a cool October afternoon. Despite it being too warm for such clothing, Case was wearing a black leather jacket.

Diggy was sipping a chocolate milkshake he'd been nursing for the past hour, and it had turned thin and watery.

"Okay, so we're here," Stick said. "What did you want to see us about?"

"Case says you guys've done good work carrying packages," Benny said.

Diggy slurped up the last drops of milkshake.

Stick grinned. "Of course. We do good work."

"I got another job if you want it."

No longer working on the shake, Diggy asked, "What kinda job?"

Benny smiled a toothy smile. "One that pays well."

"How well?" Stick asked.

"Fifty grand."

"Must be a big job," Diggy said.

"What?" Stick asked, "You want us to kill the president?"

"Not the president," Benny deadpanned.

"Wait, wait, wait," Diggy said. "You actually want us to

shoot somebody?"

"You're cops." Benny grinned. "Cops kill more people than old age."

Diggy and Stick both leaned forward and looked at one another.

Stick said, "You're cracking jokes, but this isn't funny."

"Fuck no, it ain't," Diggy agreed. "We ain't in the killin' business."

"Never mind then," Benny said. "I guess I was given bad intel."

Diggy looked at him. "What intel was that?"

"A little birdie told me you owe just under twenty thousand dollars to a bookie in Bonner Springs. A fat fuck named Finny something or other."

"Finny Saentz," Diggy said. "They call him Fat Finny."

"Funny thing, but the birdie said you bet on hockey."

"Why's that funny?"

"I never heard of a colored guy who liked hockey before."

Benny turned to Stick. "And you…"

"What about me?" Stick asked.

"I heard you were behind on your mortgage payments." Benny shrugged. "But hey, maybe I was wrong. Like I said, bad intel."

Stick stared off into the distance, weighing his options.

"I ain't sayin' we gon' do it," Diggy said, "but who is it you want clipped?"

"The guy's a pro football player," Benny said.

"He plays for KC?"

Benny nodded. "Yep."

"If you gon' go after somebody high-profile like that, the dude musta done some serious shit or he owes you a lotta bread," Diggy said.

Benny looked at him. "What's your point?"

"It's serious."

"Okay," Benny said, grinning. "I'll ask again: what's your

point?"

"That kinda job is worth more than fifty."

"Fifty is bullshit," Stick agreed. "You're right about us needing money, sure, but what we don't need is a residency on death row. And Dig is right—a job like that is going to cost more money than that."

Benny took a hit off his vape pen.

"This guy," Benny said, "he ain't high-profile. He's a second-string kicker."

Diggy shrugged. "He's still worth more than fifty."

Benny sighed and looked at Diggy. "I'll pay you dummies an even hundred if you'll do it and shut up. But that's it. Not a dime more."

Diggy and Stick leaned forward and looked at each other again.

Stick said, "I've got a question."

"I'll have an answer."

"Why us? You could have any one of your fuckheads go after the guy—"

Diggy looked at Case and chuckled. "You hear that? Sticky said you was a fuckhead."

Case just wrinkled his mouth.

"The reason I came to you two is because a cop car can get close to this spic," Benny said. "A cop car can pull this fucker's BMW over without any attention and get right up on him and pop a cap in him."

"Then why don't you just steal a cop car?" Diggy asked.

Benny looked back and forth at them. He was becoming irritated. "This is your last chance. You either take the money now or you miss out. Also, if you don't do it, you're not working for me anymore."

CHAPTER TWENTY-ONE

It was night and the air was crisp. Kansas City had just beaten Denver in a close Sunday night matchup. Diggy and Stick were sitting in their cruiser, just one more cop car in a cluster of black-and-whites outside player parking. They were parked about forty feet from the railing surrounding the player parking area. There were fans in jerseys and team jackets standing around the railing, waiting to ambush their favorite players with autograph requests.

Diggy was eating Cheerios, rustling the bag as loudly as Stick had ever heard it done, and complaining about his latest girlfriend. Stick nodded toward the parking area. "I see him."

Diggy squinted. "Where?"

"Over there, getting into his Beamer."

"You sure that's him?"

Stick said. "Viktor Barrera, momentarily alive and well."

Diggy started the ignition and said, "Looks like he's alone."

"Thank God," Stick said dryly. "I'd hate to waste too many bullets."

Diggy waited until the black vehicle was exiting before nonchalantly pulling out and following it. He was careful to stay far enough behind Barrera that they wouldn't be noticed. They followed him north on I-35 to eastbound I-75. They got right up behind him. They were near the Blue Ridge Cutoff when Diggy flipped on the blues and twos.

Seeing the flashing lights in his rearview, Barrera slowed and pulled the Beamer over and onto the shoulder. "Here goes nothin'," Diggy said as he put the cruiser in park.

Diggy and Stick climbed out. Diggy's eyes were locked on the driver's side door of the Beamer, while Stick kept an eye on the passing traffic. Diggy strode up to Barrera's window, which was already down.

Barrera squinted up at him, and Diggy and Stick were hit with the pungent aroma of weed smoke.

"You gettin' high and drivin'?" Diggy said. "You know better than that."

"It ain't no thing, man," Barrera said. "I'm a football player. We just won—"

"Shut up and gimme your license and registration," Diggy said. Diggy was hunkered down over the window and Stick was standing behind him, keeping watch. Barrera reached for this glove compartment. When the football player leaned over, Stick said, "Do it now."

Diggy stuck his Glock into the car, pressing its barrel flush against the back of Barrera's head. He squeezed the trigger, firing twice in quick succession. Diggy and Stick then turned, business as usual, and strolled back to the cruiser.

CHAPTER TWENTY-TWO

"This is my favorite part," the judge told Stick.

The clip skipped ahead to a scene with Stick talking to Benny from a pay phone.

CHAPTER TWENTY-THREE

The phone rang three times before Case picked up. "Who dis?"

"Put Benny on," Stick said.

Case chuckled. Stick didn't understand.

"Sure thing," Case said.

There was about thirty seconds of rustling before Benny got on the phone.

"Yeah?"

"It's Stick."

"Is there something you wanna tell me?" Benny asked.

"We smoked Viktor."

"You sure about that?"

"I'm sure." Stick chuckled. "Unless Viktor's tough enough to walk away from two bullets at point blank range, then yes, he's gone. His brains were all over the fucking car."

"You clowns shot the wrong guy."

Stick's jaw tightened and he tilted his head, mashing the phone receiver against his ear. "That's bullshit."

"Haven't you seen the news, Stick?"

"I was there. I don't need to."

"Guess what the news is saying?"

Stick was becoming irritated. "Are we going to play twenty questions, or are you going get to the point?"

"This point is," Benny said, "all the news channels are talking about the Kansas City football player who got popped on the side of the highway."

"So what's the problem?

"The player you killed was Hector Garza, second year tight end out of Nebraska."

Stick leaned his head down against the edge of the metal payphone frame. He closed his eyes and exhaled, biting the inside of his lip.

"You guys fucked this up," Benny said.

"So what then?"

"You dumb fucks are gonna make it right."

"How?"

"You've got to kill Viktor Barrera."

Stick felt his stomach churning and he had to choke back vomit.

"Do me one favor," Benny said.

"What?"

"Clip the right fuckin' guy this time. You dummies keep this up, Kansas City won't have enough players to finish the season."

CHAPTER TWENTY-FOUR

The Kenyan judge looked down at a piece of paper he was holding. "It says here that Viktor Barrera mysteriously disappeared a week later." He looked up at Stick with the most judgmental of judgmental expressions. "But we both know what happened to him, don't we?"

CHAPTER TWENTY-FIVE

In another room somewhere far away, the very serious judge who resembled Peter Cushing stared at Diggy. "You buried Mr. Barrera in a landfill."

Diggy stared at him, saying nothing.

Diggy leaned back in his chair with his legs stretched out, and the level to which he was relaxed irritated the judge.

"Have you no remorse, Mr. Diggs?"

"Of course I got remorse. What do I look like? Some kinda asshole?"

"I see a lot of really horrible shit here, day in and day out. But you, Mr. Diggs, are one of the most disgusting men I've ever had the misfortune of presiding over."

At that moment in a way station far away, this was happening:

"I see no reason to continue watching clips," Stick's judge said. "I've seen more than enough to make my decision."

Stick tried to talk his way out of it but to no avail.

And just like that, Diggy and Stick were sentenced to eternity in Hades.

CHAPTER TWENTY-SIX

Stick was made to strip down to his bare ass, and he was escorted into a room with white walls, ceiling, and floor.

"I hope you guys are getting your jollies looking at my cock," Stick said.

The black orderly who had led him in chuckled. "Getting my jollies by laughing at how small it is."

"Hey now."

Stick was made to stand and face a bare wall at the end of the room.

"Close your eyes, Mr. Figgers."

Stick did as he was told. As he stood with his eyes clamped shut, a laser light scanned across his body. When the laser light reached Stick's far right side, it stopped and then scanned back across his body again. It scanned and re-scanned, scanned and re-scanned, scanned and re-scanned repeatedly, and Stick's body disappeared, little by little, little by little, until he was gone.

CHAPTER TWENTY-SEVEN

Diggy felt the cold rain even before he was fully materialized. The whole transporting process took less than a minute. Once it was completed, he found himself standing naked in the middle of a dark street in pouring rain. His body was shivering before his mind could even comprehend what was happening.

"The fuck is this?" Diggy said to himself.

He was in the center of a street in an urban city he didn't recognize. A city where everything seemed to be made of concrete. With rain in his eyes, he saw a few men, each separate, staring at him from a distance. When he realized he was naked, Diggy reached down with both hands to cover his dick.

He looked through the rain at a bearded man with dark skin—not black, perhaps Middle Eastern—who was standing on the sidewalk, staring at him.

"Hey, mister!" Diggy yelled. Realizing Diggy was calling to him, the man turned and walked off into the rain. "*Hey!*" Diggy called again, but it was no use. He turned and saw that the other men who had been staring at him were also walking away.

"*Hey, buddy!*" he yelled at one of them—*any* one of them who might acknowledge him. "Where can I get some clothes? Or a fuckin' umbrella?"

No one paid him any mind. So here he was, standing buck-ass naked in the center of the street, in pouring rain, with his hands concealing his junk. He stood there for a moment, looking around, taking in his surroundings. It was a city, maybe New York City. He'd never been to New York City, but this is what it looked like in movies. But there were no cars. Then Diggy looked up and saw something for the first time—*the sky was ablaze with fire!* The fire was somehow up, higher, above the rain, *burning.*

"*What the fuck?*" He knew rain could not be falling from a sky that was on fire, and he knew the sky could not be on fire, rain or no rain. But knowing these things did nothing to change the fact that this was what he saw.

Was this Hell? If it was, it wasn't like any hell he'd ever heard of. And where was Stick? Diggy looked around, scanning the street through the rain, but saw no signs of his partner. He was shivering hard and his teeth were chattering. Knowing he had to locate some clothes quickly, he started toward the alley.

"Fuck my life," Diggy muttered.

CHAPTER TWENTY-EIGHT

As Diggy made his way down the alley, he took a step and screamed out in pain as his bare foot came down on something sharp and jagged. Diggy jumped away from the glass—he was sure it was broken glass by the way it felt—and toppled back, his back flat on the pavement. The fall was awkward and the cold, wet pavement briefly distracted from the pain in his foot.

Diggy rolled forward onto his ass and sat for a moment, trying to decide his next move. He pulled his foot up to inspect the wound. He couldn't see well in the dark alley, but he knew his foot was covered in blood. He learned that it was indeed a shard of glass, and it was sticking halfway out of the wound. He braced himself for more pain and pulled the glass out quickly, howling as he did. He held the bloody piece of glass up and looked it over before tossing it aside.

"You're new here, huh?" said a gravelly voice from up ahead, to his left. Diggy looked and saw an old white man who appeared to be homeless—*they have homeless people in Hell?*—rising to his feet behind a trash can and a smattering of trash bags.

Diggy used one arm to push himself up, still covering his dick with the other. As he did this, he kept his eyes on the man.

"I didn't see you there," Diggy said, wiping away rain from his eyes.

Diggy thought his eyes must have been growing accustomed

to the darkness as he could see the man smiling. He had a bushy white beard and one of his eyes was missing. There was no patch, no bandage, no nothing—just a nasty black socket. Taking inventory of the man's clothes, Diggy saw what looked like dried blood on his shirt and pants.

"Where am I?" Diggy asked.

The old man cackled. "Where do you think you are?"

Diggy stood there covering his dick, his foot hurting like blue fuck, and said, "I ain't sure."

"This is Hades. Some folks call it Hell."

Diggy wrinkled his brow. "This ain't like no Hell I ever seen."

The homeless man nodded. "Nothing here is like they said it would be, but it's Hell alright."

"It's dark and rainy," Diggy said. "I thought there would be fire."

The old man pointed to the sky. "There's fire up there."

"Yeah, but I thought there'd be fire everywhere, like *we* was gonna be on fire. You know, that whole gnashing of teeth stuff."

"I think they say that to fool you."

Diggy leveled his gaze at the man. "How long have you been here?"

"A long, long time," the homeless man said. "It was 1935 when I died. What year is it now?"

"Look man, I'm cold and wet," Diggy said. "You gotta tell me, where can I get some clothes?"

The old man cackled again. "This is the crazy part. Well, one of many crazy parts. There aren't enough clothes for everybody. There's a limited amount of them, and they don't allow anyone to make more. There's just enough to go around, maybe not even enough. It's hard to get clothes here, and when you get them, it's ever harder to keep them."

"Where did you get yours?"

The homeless man looked at him sheepishly. "I killed a man

my first day here."

"You killed him?"

The man nodded. "Well, they call it re-killing, but yeah, it's the same thing. I busted his head wide open with a rock. Those were different clothes, though. I've had a lot of clothes over the years." The man seemed to consider the implications of what he'd said. He looked at Diggy. "If you decide to re-kill somebody for clothes, don't re-kill me. I'm the guy who helped you."

CHAPTER TWENTY-NINE

Now dressed in the homeless man's dirty, blood-stained clothes, Diggy made his way down the sidewalk. His feet were still bare except for black dress socks, because the homeless man's feet were smaller than Diggy's. He'd tried like hell to push his feet into his shoes but couldn't do it.

The rain kept coming and Diggy wondered if it ever stopped. He couldn't imagine an eternity where it poured rain all the time. He realized now he should have asked the homeless man about this and a million other things, but it was too late now.

As he walked, searching for someone to steal shoes from, Diggy watched for Stick, but didn't see him. Looking ahead, Diggy saw a broad-chested middle-aged white man with a black beard approaching. Diggy and the man were still a good thirty feet from one another, and Diggy was eyeballing the man's brown dress shoes, trying to assess their size. As the man grew close, Diggy stepped out in front of him with his palm up.

The man stopped, irritated. "What the hell?"

"Just stop," Diggy said, staring down at his feet. "What size shoes you wear?"

This startled the man. "*What?*"

"You heard me," Diggy said, getting in his face.

"Uh...eight and a half," the man said. "I wear eight and a half."

Diggy nodded and walked past him. "Cool, cool. I need tens."

The man stood there, watching Diggy walk away. "What the hell, man?"

Diggy wheeled around and glared at him. He pointed at the man. "You best get steppin', less you wanna get fucked up."

The man *hrrumphed* and went on his way. Diggy turned in the other direction and continued his search.

CHAPTER THIRTY

Not too far away, Stick was having his own troubles finding clothing. He'd been here for what felt like thirty or forty minutes and was running naked at top speed through an alley. As he ran, it occurred to him he hadn't seen a single car. As Stick sprinted on, he spotted two men ahead, standing near a door to his left. They were smoking cigarettes in the rain, without an umbrella, and laughing. He couldn't hear what they were saying, but whatever it was, it was cracking them up.

He slowed as he approached them, slowing his run to a walk. Both men noticed him at the same time.

"Who the fuck are you supposed to be?" asked one of the men.

"Yeah," said the other. "Who you supposed to be?"

Stick approached them with his right hand covering his dick. "I just got here."

One of the guys nodded. "I see that."

"What is this place?"

The two men chuckled.

"This is Hell," the man said.

"*Hades*," the other man corrected. "Hades."

"Yeah, yeah," responded the first man. "It's the same shit, though, right?"

The second man shrugged. Stick now saw there was dried blood on the man's shirt.

Stick nodded toward the man's cigarette. "You think I can bum one of those?"

The two men stared at him for a moment, trying to decide. Finally, the first guy shrugged and said, "Sure, what the hell. They don't stay lit too good in the rain, though." He reached inside his jacket and slid a cigarette pack out from the breast pocket of his flannel shirt. He pulled a cigarette out and handed it to Stick. Stick held the cigarette to his lips, and the man leaned in to light it. When he was close, Stick smashed his forehead into the guy's nose as hard as he could. The man went reeling back. Stick's head hurt like blue fuck, but he spun on the second man and dry-gulched him, giving him a straight punch to the Adam's apple. Both men, still on their feet, were holding injured body parts, trying to regain their composure. Stick turned back to the guy he'd headbutted. There was blood in Stick's eyes, mixing with the rain, but he grabbed the guy by the sides of his head and pushed him against the wall. After the man collided with the cement wall, Stick, his hands tightly gripping each side of the guy's head, smashed it against the wall three times, *hard*. When Stick stepped back, the man fell to the slick pavement.

Stick, blood in his eyes, turned back to the Adam's apple guy, still struggling to find his breath. As Stick moved in, the guy's eyes grew saucer-like, and Stick kicked him hard in the nuts with his bare foot. As the man doubled over, Stick smashed a hard uppercut to his face. When Stick felt it connect, he knew immediately the man was out for the count.

Stick, naked as the proverbial jaybird, stood over the two unconscious men, swaying as he did. He laughed a dark laugh as he looked down on them. "You guys ever had your ass kicked by a naked man before?" Hearing his own voice, Stick snapped back into the moment and went to work removing the men's clothes.

When this was finished, Stick was wearing a combination of their clothes. He decided to go commando and skip wearing underwear since he wasn't keen on wearing another man's drawers. He wore the broad-shouldered man's clothes, including the black jacket and red flannel shirt, and the other man's shoes, which fit fairly well. He stood in the rain for a moment, admiring his clothes. He started to leave and stopped himself. He'd forgotten something. He crouched down and picked the lighter and the pack of cigarettes up off the ground.

As he did, he heard a man's voice from about ten feet away say, "Good thinking. You never know when you'll need a smoke."

CHAPTER THIRTY-ONE

Once Stick's body was standing erect again, he saw a tough-looking man with a thick black mustache and shiny, slicked-back hair, standing there. He was surrounded by half a dozen other tough-looking bastards. The man nodded toward the incapacitated men on the ground. "They dead?"

"Everyone here is dead," Stick said.

The man rolled his eyes and looked at his lackeys. "We've got a wiseass here, fellas." He turned back to Stick. "Allow me to rephrase the goddamn question. Have you re-killed them?"

"I don't think so, but I don't see how it's any of your business."

The man smiled. "Seeing how I'm these two sonsofbitches' boss, and how you just beat the bloody piss out of them behind my bar, I'd say it's my business."

Stick's body tensed and he prepared for the expected attack. He balled his hands into fists. The man's gaze dropped to Stick's clenched fists, and his smile broadened. "There's no need for that," the man said, stepping forward and reaching out his hand for Stick to shake. Stick looked at it, unsure, but shook it.

"Name's Swearengen," the man said. "Al Swearengen. What's yours?"

"Dwayne Figgers," Stick said. "People call me Stick."

"Well, Stick," the man said, "I'm damn pleased to meet you."

CHAPTER THIRTY-TWO

In the days to come—it was hard to know how many since it was always nighttime—Diggy learned a lot about Hades. He did this by observing things and by striking up conversations with a number of men, all of whom were guarded and on their toes, which told him a lot about Hades in itself. There were other things he figured out on his own, like the fact you didn't perspire in Hades.

Hades looked like Earth, other than the swirling fire in the sky and the existence of what he was told were a number of hideous creatures that didn't exist back home. Diggy hadn't seen the worst of them himself, but the young heavyset black man who told him about them seemed horrified recounting them. At first, as the kid told him about dragons and similar creatures in Hades, Diggy thought he was being sold a bullshit story. But as the story progressed, he had seen on the kid's face and heard in his words that he was telling the truth. A day or so later, Diggy saw his first *ballywonk*, although he didn't yet know the word. He'd seen a man walking down the street with a dog-sized lizard on a leash. The lizard's mouth was open, exposing giant, sharp-as-fuck teeth, and its head and tail thrashed from side to side. Having never seen such a creature before, Diggy had become genuinely frightened and vowed to steer clear of these creatures.

In Hades, there was nothing but city—one long, unending

urban landscape stretching across a seemingly endless expanse. A guy told him it was supposed to look like downtown Times Square in the late 1970s.

"How the hell does that work?" Diggy asked, wiping rain out of his eyes.

The young man tilted his head in confusion. "Whatchu mean?"

"I'm assuming Hades has always existed."

"Well," said the young man, "not quite, but for a million years or so."

"Okay," Diggy said, "how does that work? How could a place that's a million years old look so much like a place that only existed for a brief time fifty years ago?"

The young man's face lit up with understanding. "Oh, I got ya," he said. "I asked that same thing to a man when I first got here. This was in 1983, mind you, and he'd been told that Times Square was actually made to look like Hades, but I don't know how that would work either. We didn't really talk about it anymore after that, and I got the feeling the old guy who was telling me didn't really know what he was talking about."

"There are men like that here?" Diggy had asked.

"There's men like that everywhere there are men."

In his first week or so—again, he couldn't be sure exactly how long it was—Diggy also learned that Hades had some of the comforts of home, like cigarettes, dope, and whiskey. Strangely enough, there was no drinkable water—only whiskey. As for water, the rain could not be collected. Diggy tried multiple times to catch water in his hands, but it seemed to dissipate immediately. He even tried turning his head skyward with his mouth open, but somehow no water ever reached his mouth. Diggy liked whiskey as much as anyone, but he couldn't imagine drinking only whiskey for all eternity.

A second and third gentleman confirmed what the homeless man had said—that there was a finite amount of clothing, making clothing invaluable. So valuable, in fact, that men sometimes killed for them. This, of course, led to another question: if a man was "killed" in Hades—or *re-killed*—where did he go? Diggy asked a couple of men about this. The young man who told him about the Times Square being made to resemble Hades, said, "They say you go to a place that's way worse than here."

Diggy stared at him through the falling rain. "How's it worse?"

The young man rubbed his head. "I don't know, but that's what they say."

"Maybe," Stick said, "you just die and all this shit ends once and for all."

"Nah," the young man said. "That ain't it. It just gets worse and worse. It's like that Dante 'circles of Hell' shit, with each circle being worse than the last."

"But nobody knows?"

"Well," the young man said, grinning, "the guys who get re-killed and sent there know, but they ain't tellin' nobody."

As for re-killing people, there was a notable distinction to make: in Hades, there were no guns. So if you re-killed someone, it took work to do it. You had to use knives, blunt instruments, or your bare hands.

There were no umbrellas in Hades. He'd guessed that since he hadn't seen any, but it was still frustrating to hear it confirmed. Also, there were no automobiles in Hades. No bicycles, no transportation of any kind. The rain was another thing—as Diggy had suspected, it never, ever stopped. Diggy conversed with an old Korean man who had been in Hades for hundreds of years, who told him he'd never seen a single minute without rain in all the time he'd been there. Talking to the Korean man brings up another thing Diggy learned—everyone in Hades spoke the same language. When you spoke, you heard your native tongue. But everyone who heard it understood it in their language.

About two days into his sentence in Hades, Diggy concluded

that the place wasn't so bad. He didn't love it, but it really wasn't as bad as they told you it would be back home. This conclusion momentarily brought him joy.

That was before he realized there were no women.

CHAPTER THIRTY-THREE

After another day or so, or at least what he *believed* to be another day or so, Diggy realized that he hadn't seen a single woman since he'd arrived in Hades. Where were the women?

That was the day he spoke to the old Korean man. They were sitting on a park bench, conversing in the pouring rain, and the Korean was telling him things about Hades. He was telling him about how he would encounter men from all time periods here, and thus would see clothing from all lands and periods, when Diggy interrupted.

"I'm sorry to interrupt you, but I got a question," Diggy said.

"What is your question?"

Diggy leaned in toward him, both his eyes and mouth smiling. "I been here a few days now, and I ain't seen one woman. *Not one!* So I been tryin'a figure it out..." As he spoke, the Korean's lips stretched into a smile.

The old man sighed, his smile disappearing, and he stared off into the distance. "I hate to tell you this, but there are no women."

Diggy leaned back a little, his eyes big, looking like he'd just been smacked in the face with a shovel. *"Whatchu mean no women?"*

The old man looked at him with an apologetic expression. "I'm sorry. There are no women in Hades. I wish there were, but..."

Diggy stared at him, trying to understand. "So you're tellin' me I ain't never gonna have sex again?"

"Well," the old man said, "you might have sex, but it won't be with a woman."

CHAPTER THIRTY-FOUR

Stick was sitting at a wooden table in Swearengen's bar, the Gem, drinking whiskey. Swearengen sat across from him. His goons were scattered about, sitting on bar stools and whatnot. The two men Stick had obliterated out back had been carried off.

"How's the drink?" Swearengen asked.

Stick took another drink. After swallowing, he said, "This stuff'll kill you."

Swearengen raised an eyebrow. "You said everyone was already dead."

Stick grinned. "*Touché.*"

"Everyone is dead here, but they can be re-killed," Swearengen said. "Thing is, there's a sort of honor among thieves here. We try not to kill each other if we can help it."

Stick had surmised that Swearengen was a criminal of some sort, so he asked, "So what do you do?"

Swearengen blinked. "What do you mean?"

"When you have to...*deal* with someone."

"We're real big on torture."

"Torture?"

"You are familiar with the concept, are you not?"

Stick nodded. "I know what torture is. I was just trying to wrap my head around it." He paused for a moment, looking down at the table, thinking. He raised his head to look at his host. "If you can die, but you're already in Hell—"

"*Hades*," Swearengen corrected.

"Potato potahto, same shit, different toilet…"

"Anyway," Swearengen said, "you were saying?"

"If you can be killed here, then what happens to you after that?"

Swearengen sat back, his eyes big, his lips to the side of his mouth. "We call it *re-killing* when someone gets killed here. As to where you go from here, damned if I know. No one knows for sure. All we know is that it's someplace worse." He met Stick's gaze. "Can you imagine that? Someplace shittier than this?"

Thinking about the darkness and the pouring rain, Stick shook his head.

"At least it ain't fire," Swearengen said. "I just knew I was going to be facing an eternity of hell fire."

"But instead you got this."

Swearengen nodded glumly. "Instead I got this."

"I've got some questions about this place."

Swearengen grinned. "Everybody's got questions, and they're always the same, so I'll just save you the questioning and answer them for you now."

Swearengen laid it all out for Stick, at least everything he could think of at the moment. He explained to Stick that Hades was one giant metropolis, controlled by thousands of crime lords. Swearengen was one of them. Every one of these chieftains had his own gang that oversaw their geographical areas and the crime that occurred within it. Swearengen told him there were no guns in Hades, which made re-killing even more of a pain in the ass for anyone wanting to do it.

"So you haven't killed anyone since you've been here?" Stick asked.

There was a glint in Swearengen's eyes and his mouth curled into a smirk. "I never said that. I just said we try to avoid it."

Swearengen explained that there were no automobiles in Hades. Even though Swearengen had never seen an automobile himself before having died in 1904, he knew about them because this was a question people frequently asked. But, he explained, there was said to be one automobile, although he'd never actually seen it. That one belonged to Satan.

"Satan's got a car?" Stick asked.

Swearengen nodded. "That's what they say."

"No cars and no guns," Stick said dryly. "What fun is that?"

Swearengen grinned a shit-eating grin. "Trust me, there are worse things that we don't have."

"Like what?"

"Brace yourself, boy."

"Consider me braced."

"In your time here in Hades, is there anything you haven't seen?"

Stick didn't understand.

"Think hard," Swearengen said.

Stick wracked his brain, but he didn't know.

Swearengen leaned in toward Stick as if he was telling him a secret. "Women," he said. "There's no pussy here."

Stick's jaw dropped. *"None?"*

"None. That's what makes this place hell."

"Hades," Stick corrected.

"It's enough to drive a man insane."

"So what then?" Stick asked. "Women don't go to hell?"

Swearengen sat way back in his chair again and shrugged. "No one knows. At least no one here. There's a rumor that there's a separate place for women, but that has yet to be proven."

"Ain't that a bitch?" Stick said.

Swearengen said. "Quite the opposite, in fact."

CHAPTER THIRTY-FIVE

Diggy was, at least for the moment, a homeless man himself, wandering the streets in the rain, searching for shelter and money to get by. In Hades, the currency consisted of thick gold (were they gold? Diggy didn't know for sure) coins called gerro. Diggy figured one gerro was worth about the same as a dollar was back home. He suspected there were larger forms of currency than a gerro, but he had yet to see them. Everything he'd seen had been priced in an even number of gerros, so there was no change given after a transaction.

Being homeless, or what Diggy considered homeless, in Hades was something altogether different. A lot of people here didn't have homes. The wealthy and the damned lucky had apartments where they could be alone, but many didn't have that luxury. Besides, even if a man had his own place, there wasn't much to do there besides think and sleep or drink and get high. The drug of choice here looked like a joint—not a blunt, no one here smoked those—and was called kamur.

Diggy learned quickly that bars didn't like gerro-less men hanging around, and he was kicked out of several. There were no restaurants in Hades, only bars. The reason for this should have been obvious after the first day or so, but there was no eating in the afterlife. There was only drinking. As such, Diggy no longer had bowel movements. He still pissed, but he didn't shit, which was fine by him as he didn't miss it. But there were things he did miss.

He missed the company of women, he missed his family, and he missed his crazy-ass friend Stick. But those last two things, family and Stick, were really one and the same, and Diggy was more aware of that now than he'd ever been before. As he roamed the streets, finding momentary reprieve from the rain wherever he could, he begged for gerros and searched for Stick. He wondered if Stick was even here. Maybe Stick had been sent to some other, far away version of Hell. That would make sense. What else would Hell be but a place where you lost everything you cared about?

Diggy was sitting on a bench in the rain and darkness when he saw a well-dressed middle-aged white man who looked either American, English, or Canadian. Diggy didn't know and didn't care. The man walked toward him, and Diggy thought maybe he was a do-gooder wanting to help. Diggy stood and said, "I hate to ask, mister, but could you spare a gerro or two?"

The man eyed him incredulously. Some looks threw daggers; this man's threw dog shit.

"You make me sick," the man said. He didn't even have the decency to step back and be wary, which offended Diggy greatly.

The two men were close now, less than a foot away from one another.

Diggy cocked his head and gave the man his most vicious look. *The fuck you say to me?*

"You heard me," the man said. "Men like you make me sick. You're trash. Worse than trash. Everyone starts out here with nothing. But most men—*decent men*—work their way up so they can have nicer clothing, self-respect, and dignity. But others—*lazy bums like you*—wander the streets and mooch off others, doing nothing to help yourself."

This caught Diggy off guard. "You don't know me."

Diggy was close to punching him but hadn't done it simply because he'd been shocked by the man's audacity. But then the man spat in his face, and Diggy roared to life and went to work, delivering blow after blow to his head. The man was unconscious the second Diggy's first punch connected, but Diggy took all his frustrations out on him.

This would be a memorable day for Diggy. It would be the day he obtained the man's nice, dapper clothing, as well as his snazzy lizard shoes. But the thing he liked most out of all the things he stole from the man was the pocketful of money.

CHAPTER THIRTY-SIX

For the first time, Diggy saw currency other than a gerro—there were ten small blue metal squares in the pockets of the stolen jacket. Diggy guessed the squares to be currency because they bore the same logo as the gerros. But he couldn't be sure. Maybe the squares weren't money at all. And if they were, he had no idea what their value was. He figured he'd just amble into a bar to have a drink, and he would offer the bartender one of the squares as payment. If the barman balked, he'd know he'd made a mistake and would then pay with the loose gerros that were also in the pocket of his new jacket.

Walking down the street in his sharp new threads, wet as they were, Diggy felt like a million bucks. Or, as the "when in Rome" folks might say, a million gerros.

Things were looking up.

CHAPTER THIRTY-SEVEN

Stick had been working for Al Swearengen for some time now. Probably a month or so by the old Earth standard. There was no way to know how long since it was always nighttime, and there was no measurement of time in Hades.

Stick hadn't wanted to work for anyone. He'd only wanted to find Diggy, but Swearengen had convinced him. Stick had nowhere to go and nothing else to do. Without Swearengen, he would have no gerros and no shelter. It seemed to Stick that having a purpose was an important part of coping with his new realities. And since almost every man in Hades worked for one crime boss or another, Stick figured Swearengen was as good as the next.

Swearengen had taken a shine to him. Stick didn't know why, but the man saw similarities between Stick and himself. Stick could not see any similarities between them beyond their both being bastards, but if the idea suited the boss, then so be it.

Stick had gone to work for the man, not knowing what exactly that work might be. When he'd asked Swearengen, he'd told him "beating people up, bouncing in the bar, shit like that." Stick figured beating people up was something he had a talent for, so sure, that would be fine.

But then, not long after Stick had come onboard, Swearengen asked him to complete a different kind of task. Sitting in the back corner booth at the Gem, Swearengen had looked at him with his damnable grin and said, "I've got a job for you, Sticky boy."

"What kind of work?"

Swearengen's grin spread and Stick saw that gleam in his eye again. It seemed to Stick that that twinkle only appeared in his eye when he was up to something bad.

"I need you to take care of a fella for me," Swearengen said.

Stick nodded. "How bad you want him beaten?"

"Not a beating. Not this time."

"Then what?"

"Use your imagination."

Meeting Swearengen's gaze, Stick asked, *"Torture?"*

"No," Swearengen said grimly. "Not torture."

"Then what?"

"More."

Stick looked at him, considering this. "I thought you said you didn't kill people here."

Swearengen's grin transformed into something more mischievous. "You heard me, but you didn't *listen.* I didn't say we never kill, and the proper term is *re-kill* by the way. I said we *try* never to kill."

"Only in extreme cases?"

Swearengen nodded. "Sometimes you've got to re-kill a man. Sometimes there's just no other way. Look around. This is an entire world with nothing but dirty, rotten, no-account cocksuckers, all of 'em evil to their core. That honor-among-thieves goodwill shit only goes so far."

"Then you've got to re-kill them," Stick said, understanding now.

Leaning over the table, Swearengen opened his palms. "Then you've got to do it. Hell, the bastards *make* you re-kill them."

"I don't know," Stick said. "I'm tired of killing."

"I'll make it worth your while if you do this."

"How?"

"Three things, Stick, my boy."

"I'm all ears."

"First, I'll make you my private bodyguard while you're here," Swearengen said. "That's an important job."

"What else?"

"I'll help you find the man you came here to get."

"Dread Corbin," Stick said.

"But the third reason is the reason you'll do it for."

"What's that?"

Swearengen took another drink of his whiskey. Then he wiped his lips with the back of his hand. When he was finished, he returned his gaze to Stick and winked. "I'll introduce you to the Oracle, my boy."

"I'll want to meet the Oracle?" Stick asked.

"Oh yes. You'll most definitely want to meet the Oracle."

CHAPTER THIRTY-EIGHT

Once Swearengen had explained the Oracle, Stick wholeheartedly agreed to re-kill the man. The guy Swearengen wanted re-killed was an Irishman named Davey O'Connell. O'Connell had sold kamur for Swearengen but had then double-crossed him and taken off with the drugs.

"I'll tell you something, Stick," Swearengen said. "Always follow your gut."

"Yeah?"

"When I brought O'Connell into the fold, my gut was telling me he was a piece of shit like you wouldn't believe."

"Everyone in Hades is a piece of shit, though."

Swearengen grinned and nodded. "This is true, my boy, but some pieces of shit are bigger, smellier pieces of shit than others."

"I take it O'Connell is one of those?"

"You take it right. To be honest, it was stupidity on my part. O'Connell used to work for one of the other bosses, a fella named Hitler. When—"

Stick raised his palm up in front of Swearengen. "Wait, wait, wait. Back up. Did you say *Hitler*?"

Swearengen nodded. "I hear he was pretty terrible on Earth."

Stick chuckled and went to work pouring himself another whiskey. "He was more than terrible. He was the *worst*. There's not a person on Earth who doesn't know who Adolf Hitler is.

And that's saying something considering the sonofabitch has been worm food for eighty years."

"Okay," Swearengen said sternly. "Are you gonna let me finish my goddamn story, or you gonna go on giving me a history lesson?"

Stick smiled. "My bad. Go ahead."

"Thank you very fucking much," Swearengen said. "Now, O'Connell had been one of Hitler's top dogs. High up on the totem pole. Not at the very top, mind you, but pretty fucking high. So he got into a tiff, said the wrong thing or something or other, and Hitler put him back on the street." Swearengen, half drunk, put his finger up. "I shoulda known right there. I shoulda listened to my gut."

"But you didn't."

Swearengen gave him a look of toleration. "But I didn't." He paused. "I figured, how big a deal could it have been since Hitler allowed the guy to live. Hitler's a huge asshole, so it would not be hard to anger a prick like that. It could have been something small, you know? But a guy I know—a Chinaman named Dak— came to me as an intermediary and told me O'Connell was looking for work and he's a good guy, blah, blah, blah, can he come work for me?"

Stick was about to say "so you did" conversationally but caught himself.

"And the rest, as they say…"

"Is history," Stick said.

Swearengen nodded. "Fucking history."

"So you want me to re-kill him."

"Bright boy, Sticky. You must have got all A's and B's in school. Yes, you daft fuck, I want you to re-kill the cocksucker and send him on to the next level."

Stick had finished his glass while Swearengen was talking, so Swearengen refilled their empty glasses. He then held his up to Stick, who raised his, and announced, "A toast."

"What are we toasting?" Stick asked. "The death of Mr.

O'Connell?"

"Fuck no," Swearengen said. "We're toasting the beginning of yours and mine's long and prosperous relationship."

CHAPTER THIRTY-NINE

Stick felt wetter than he could remember having ever felt before. He was walking down Millicent Street, a good nine miles from the Gem. As he walked, he realized the rain never changed. It never rained more, and it never rained less. It was always the same, and it was always a pain in the ass.

Watching the buildings, looking for the place he'd been told O'Connell was, he thought he'd found it. He stood there for a long moment, staring up at the concrete building, trying to determine whether it was the right place. He finally concluded it was and approached the building's double-door entrance.

He reached into his coat pocket and wrapped his fingers around the knife he'd been given for the job. It was a strange knife, much different from anything he'd seen back home. The knife was made of a green crystal. It was beautiful, actually, but the reason Stick had come was not so beautiful. He'd asked for a gun. He'd never carried out a hit with a knife before, let alone a knife made of clear green crystal. But Swearengen had reminded him there were no guns in Hades, which Stick still couldn't believe. After all, everything here looked like a carbon copy of things on Earth, only with a handful of weird exceptions. Stick had asked Swearengen why nobody in Hades had thought to simply create their own automobiles and guns and televisions. This had caused the broad-chested man to chuckle.

Swearengen had pointed to the sky. "We can't make things

like that because the fuckers up there won't let us."

Swearengen had then explained that, although there were no cameras in Hades, the "controllers" saw everything everyone did. To this, Stick had interrupted and asked if the "controllers" used this power to bring justice to criminals. This had made Swearengen laugh *really* hard. "Think about what you're saying, Sticky, old boy. Everyone here is a criminal. Everything everyone does here is crime. They don't care about crime of any kind. At least not the kind of crime you're used to back home. Here, the only crime is trying to make contraband like clothing or guns or clocks. And trying to escape." When Stick had pressed Swearengen to tell him about the controllers, Swearengen just said, "Satan runs everything here, just like the book said. Everything else about Hades might have been wrong, but they got that part right. Hades is filled with bosses...men like myself. But Satan is the top boss. Everyone answers to him."

Clutching the knife, Stick pushed the glass door open. There were no photographs in Hades, so all Stick had to identify O'Connell by was Swearengen's description that he was "a big bald Irish motherfucker." The description wasn't overly specific, but Stick figured it would be enough for him to identify the guy.

There was no one in the small front room. There was only a checkered tile floor and a set of stairs on his right. Stick had expected an elevator, but of course, there wasn't one. Maybe elevators were another luxury not permitted in Hades. As Stick started up the stairs, he wondered if the controllers would punish someone for building an elevator.

By the time he reached the seventh floor, where Swearengen's informant told him O'Connell was hiding, Stick was panting hard and out of breath. There was no movement on the floor, which consisted of ten apartments, so Stick decided it would be best for him to stop to catch his breath. He stood there for a moment, composing himself. Once he felt well enough to carry out the job, he made his way down the hall to room 706. Standing there staring at the door, Stick considered his options.

Should he knock? No, probably not. That would alert O'Connell.

Stick stepped in front of the door and squared his stance, preparing to kick the door in. He had the crystal knife out in front of him, ready to attack. Stick took a deep breath, thinking, *Here goes nothing.* Momentarily shifting all his weight back onto his left foot, he raised his right, leaning forward and kicking it into the door as he had so many times as a cop. But the door didn't break. Stick's foot bounced off, hurting like blue fuck, and making a considerable ruckus. All this happened in about two seconds, and Stick was simultaneously hurting, trying to find his footing, and trying to understand what had just happened.

The door swung open and a big, burly, bald Irishman in a gray suit stood there, poised to attack. Stick pushed through the pain and lunged at the big bastard, who greeted him with a fist to the side of the head. Luckily, the punch only grazed Stick, who jammed his knife into the man's throat, causing a geyser of blood to erupt. Despite this, the man grabbed Stick, wrapping his thick arms around his body, trying to crush him like a python. Losing his breath and feeling himself being crushed in the man's arms, Stick swung the knife upwards, burying its crystal blade in the man's stomach. Stick then yanked the blade down, causing the man's intestines to fall to the floor. But the man didn't release him immediately. It took a moment, but the man finally let go and dropped to his knees. Once he was there, Stick jammed the blood-soaked blade deep into his eye. As Stick pulled it out and the man toppled over in the doorway, he could see another big, husky bald Irishman standing a few feet behind.

What in blue fuck? Sticky thought. The man he'd killed was only a goon. Stick was exhausted, but once again pushed through it, climbing up and over the first man's body. The remaining bald man put his fists out in front of him, ready to box. Being a fighter himself, Stick welcomed this. He would make quick work of the man.

"Swearengen send you?" the man growled.

Stick said nothing. Instead, he rushed the bastard, trying to stab him. Stick liked to box and knew it could eventually come to that, but he knew it was safer to try the knife first. The big bastard ducked the blade and came up with a hard uppercut that caught Stick in his ribs. Stick moaned in pain and took a step back. He shook off the pain and locked eyes on the man.

"I'll kill you and ten more fuck monkeys just like you," the man growled.

Stick grinned despite the situation. "There's no one else like me."

The big man didn't laugh. Instead, he tried a jab, which Stick avoided easily. As the man followed through, his fist passing Stick's head, Stick's arm shot forward, jamming the green blade into his cheek. Because of the location of the wound, the blade didn't go very deep. The man's eyes grew large and he stepped back, causing the blade in Stick's hand to pull loose from the wound. The big fucker stood there for a moment, trying to shake off the pain. He looked at Stick with pure unadulterated hate in his eyes. Then, suddenly, he rushed toward Stick at full speed. Stick stepped sideways, managing to avoid him other than a brush, and the man, having prepared himself for a collision, lost his footing and fell forward onto the floor. Seeing his opportunity, Stick moved quickly and plunged the blade down hard into his back. The man's body rocked, and with the blade still in his back, he turned to his side.

"You dumb cunt," the man growled.

Stick moved quickly, getting himself in position where the big man's head was just in front of his feet. Stick raised his right foot, still hurting, and brought it down hard, smashing his heel into the side of the man's head. Then he raised his foot again and brought it down even harder this time, crushing the man's skull.

Stick stood there, swaying from exhaustion and admiring his work. Then he heard a voice from an adjoining room to his right. Completely worn out, Stick turned to see a third bald Irishman in a suit standing there, staring at him. The man cracked his knuckles and nodded for Stick to approach. "What are you waiting for?" the man asked.

CHAPTER FORTY

Stick stood there for a moment, staring at him.

"What, they got a factory somewhere that makes bald-headed Irish fucks?"

The man's menacing grin sent a chill down Stick's spine.

Stick set his feet and took a breath, still staring at him. It was now or never, he thought. Stick leaned forward and charged headlong toward the man at top speed. Unfortunately, the bald bastard had the same thought at the same moment and broke into a sprint head-first toward Stick. By the time the two men realized what was happening, it was too late. They collided hard, smashing their heads into one another. The impact rocked them both, knocking them back. Immense pain filled Stick's head, and he nearly lost his footing. He wobbled for a moment, blood in his eyes. He used his damp sleeve to wipe away the blood and saw the bald bastard do the same. He was wobbling, too.

With his head lowered some, peering upward at the man, Stick asked, "Are you Davey O'Connell?"

The man stood there, still swaying and looking every bit as tired as Stick felt, and gave him a funny look. Without taking his eyes away from Stick's, the man pointed at the first man Stick had killed. "That's Davey over there in the doorway."

"I came for him," Stick said. "Not you."

Stick started to turn, and the man said, "You're just gonna

take my word for it, just like that?"

But he wasn't. In that moment, Stick rammed his head into the man's body with all the strength he could muster, pushing him back. The move caught the man off guard, so his body was relaxed when Stick hit him. Stick allowed the momentum to carry them, and he kept pushing the man, pushing him all the way back to the window. The man made a sound, and Stick thought he was going to plead for his life, but a second later the man went crashing through the glass. Stick was barely able to stop himself from going out the window with him. As he watched, the bald man waved his arms wildly and his eyes grew to the size of golf balls. A second passed before the man started to scream, but the scream was immediately stopped by the pavement.

Looking down at the dead man's body, Stick wondered which of the bald fuckers was actually O'Connell. Momentarily distracted, Stick didn't hear the door push open in the next room. However, he did hear the ferocious, blood-curdling growl that followed.

CHAPTER FORTY-ONE

Stick's breath caught, and he spun, seeing a creature unlike anything he had seen before, stalking toward him. It was some sort of lizard, obviously O'Connell's pet, and it stood on four legs and was roughly the same size as a full-grown black Lab. It had a long, scaly tail that swept back and forth like an alligator's, and it seemed to sweep harder with each growl. Its teeth were bared—the sharpest, pointiest teeth Stick had ever laid eyes on—and it looked ready to pounce at any second. That would be no good, because if the teeth didn't kill him, Stick thought its razor-sharp claws would.

Stick reached his hand out toward the creature.

"Good doggie," he offered.

This only made the beast growl more aggressively.

"Do you do tricks?" Stick asked in something just above a whisper. "Can you roll over and fetch?"

The creature snarled viciously.

Stick tried not to move, and his eyes scanned the room, looking for something he could wield as a weapon, but there was nothing close. He looked at the creature again and saw its hind leg muscles tense up, and he knew he was out of time. In that millisecond, the beast sprung toward him. Stick ducked to his left, managing to get mostly out of its way, but its claws still ripped into his right shoulder as it sailed past. As the beast's momentum continued to carry it away from him, Stick quickly scrambled for the knife. He leaned down low to the floor, snatching it up and following through with a roll. Now face up and on his back, Stick had a good view of the creature, which had turned around, and was now coming back. The creature snarled and launched at him again. In the brief second it was in the air and hovering over him, Stick thrust the green blade upwards, into its chest. The beast let out a pained yelp, and the blade tore its flesh from chest to abdomen as its momentum propelled it forward.

The ungodly weight of the beast fell on Stick, nearly crushing him, and knocking the wind out of him. Its claws ripped into his chest. It was thrashing and, thankfully, its snarling head was above Stick's, keeping those sharp teeth away from him. Stick slid the knife out of the sticky wound and maneuvered his right arm so he could reach the beast's neck. As the creature continued to thrash, Stick jammed the blade into its throat with all the force he could muster. The thrashing increased for the briefest of moments, accompanied by a dying screech, and then the creature fell limp. Leaving the knife sticking out of the beast's throat, Stick pushed the heavy carcass off of him.

"I guess you can do a trick," Stick said wearily. "You can play dead."

CHAPTER FORTY-TWO

When Stick got to the Gem, tired and beaten to hell, Swearengen took one look at the bloody rips in his shirt and remarked, "I take it you've encountered your first ballywonk."

Stick had looked at him blankly. "What the hell is a bally-wonk?"

They were standing by the bar, and Swearengen had pointed at Stick's bloodied chest. "I assumed that's what did all this damage, judging from your wounds."

When Swearengen saw Stick's already blank look somehow become even more blank, he lowered his flattened hand to his side. "About yay big, about the size of a dog? Ugly, scaly bastard with big teeth, bigger claws, and an even bigger mean streak?"

Stick nodded wearily. "Then yeah, it was a bally-whatever you said."

"Was it wild? Roaming the streets?"

"No," Stick said. "It was inside that Irish fuck's apartment."

"You know," Swearengen said, "there are packs of wild ballywonks roaming the streets in some parts of Hades."

This startled Stick. *"Packs?"*

"As in plural. Plural ballywonks."

"I know what pack means," Stick said. "I'm just surprised to hear that there are a lot of these things roaming around out there."

"Too damned many."

Swearengen then turned and nodded to the bartender, a Japanese man named Sho. Sho poured them drinks. When Sho slid the two glasses toward Swearengen, Swearengen turned and handed one to the battle-bloodied Stick.

Stick took it, downed it in one gulp, and said, "I need to sit. I fought three big Irishmen and that...that...*ballywonk*, and I'm as tired as a one-legged man in an ass kicking contest."

"You look like that one-legged man kicked your ass," Swearengen said.

He turned to Sho, asked for the bottle, and he and Stick went back to Swearengen's booth. They sat and Stick downed another drink.

Swearengen looked at him, grinning. "Rough day?"

Stick looked up after setting his glass down. "Hardest day I've ever had." Then he reconsidered. "Well, except for the day I was forced to shoot myself in the head. That was a pretty fucking bad day, too."

Swearengen chuckled. "But you got him?"

"O'Connell?"

"Yes, O'Connell."

Stick nodded. "I re-killed him and two other big bastards who looked just like him."

"Two more O'Connells?"

Stick just nodded, pouring himself another drink. "Now what?"

"What do you mean 'now what'?"

Stick met the man's gaze. "I mean now what."

"You work for me a little longer and you earn that trip to meet the Oracle," Swearengen said. "Then, after that, I'll help you find the fella you came here to find."

"And after that?"

Swearengen shrugged and spread his hands on the table. "It's early yet. Who knows? But I can tell you what I'd like to see happen."

"A pretty blonde with big tits mysteriously shows up and

climbs on top of your cock?"

Swearengen chuckled. "Don't I wish," he said. "Don't I fucking wish. What I'd like to see happen after that is that you come back here and keep working for me. You're a tough fucker, Sticky boy, and frankly, I could use a tough fucker around here."

Seeing that Stick was considering this, Swearengen said, "It's not like you're going anywhere. We're here for fucking eternity, for Christ's sake. And if you've got to be part of someone's crew, you can be part of mine. I'll treat you good. Not as good as that blonde with the big tits, but good enough. You'll have a home and all the comforts this place allows. Now given, it doesn't allow much, but the most is a damn sight better than less, am I wrong?"

Stick saw the logic in staying on. "No," he said. "I don't think you're wrong."

As Stick spoke, Swearengen looked at the bar with a curious expression.

"Now who the fuck is this black bastard?"

Stick turned and looked at the black man in the sharp white suit standing in front of the bar. "That black bastard's name is Bobby Diggs, but his friends call him Diggy."

CHAPTER FORTY-THREE

Sho set Diggy's drink on the counter.

Diggy picked it up and eyed it suspiciously. "This glass is dirty as hell."

Sho grinned. "All the glasses are dirty. Take it or leave it."

Diggy shrugged and downed the whiskey. He set the glass back on the bar. "Gimme another."

"You haven't paid for the first."

"Put it on my tab."

Sho eyed Diggy as suspiciously as Diggy had eyed the dirty glass. "You don't have a tab."

Diggy gave him a shoulders-only shrug. "Why don't you go on and gimme one then."

"That's not how it works," Sho said. "No tabs in the Gem."

Diggy shrugged again and reached into his pocket, pulling out one of the blue squares. He plopped it down on the counter.

Sho's eyes grew large. He picked up the blue square and held it up in front of his eyes. "We don't see many of these around here."

"No shit?" Diggy asked.

Sho shook his head.

"How many drinks you figure it'll cover?" Diggy asked.

Sho looked at him and blinked. "A *rooley*? Are you kidding? It'll buy more drinks than you could drink in a month."

"I thought they didn't have months here," Diggy said.

"But you are aware of what a month is, right?"

Diggy grinned. "Drinks for the house then!"

He'd always wanted to say that.

Sho's face lit up, and he smiled. "You got it." He turned and started pouring drinks.

Diggy was about to tell him to pour his drink first but was stopped by a voice that came from his left. "We don't serve your kind here."

Diggy squinted his eyes angrily and turned to face the voice. When he did, he saw Stick standing there smiling. Swearengen was a couple steps behind.

Diggy grinned. "Ain't you a sight for sore eyes."

The two friends hugged, and Stick patted Diggy's back. Then they pulled back to look at each other.

"Where'd you get the spiffy threads?" Stick asked, checking out Diggy's pristine white suit. "I haven't seen clothes like that the whole time I been here."

Diggy tilted his head, a gleam in his eye and a big shit-eating grin on his face. "You know how Diggy do, son. Stylin', profilin'."

Swearengen's voice spoke up from behind Stick. "There's not even a drop of blood on that suit. How the hell'd you pull that off?"

Diggy looked at Swearengen. Then he looked at Stick quizzically.

"He's alright," Stick assured him. "This is Al Swearengen. He owns this place."

Offering his hand for Diggy to shake, Swearengen said, "And the boss of this organization, I might add."

Diggy's hand was already halfway extended when he heard this, and he stopped. "Whatchu mean *organization*?"

"I'll explain it all to you later," Stick said. "But Swearengen's on the level."

Diggy shook the man's hand. "Any friend of Stick is a friend 'a mine."

"Good," Swearengen said. "Come on back and join us at

our booth."

Diggy nodded, and Stick asked, "How'd you find me?"

"It wasn't that hard," Diggy said. "I just went from bar to bar, askin' everyone if they'd seen a big goofy-lookin' white dude. Told 'em you was the goofiest-lookin' perckerwood I ever saw, and they all pointed me in this direction."

"Aw, shucks," Stick said. "You say the sweetest things."

"Drinks on the house!" Sho announced. "Compliments of the black fella."

Diggy looked back at the booth where Swearengen and Stick had been sitting. Seeing only a single half-full bottle on the table, Diggy turned back to the bartender. "You better gimme another bottle. I don't think one is gonna cut it."

Sho smiled big and grabbed a bottle, handing it across the bar to Diggy. "I'll tell you what," Diggy said, "whatever's left of that square—"

"The rooley?"

"Yeah, yeah," Diggy said. "The rooley. Whatever's left of that, you can keep."

Sho's eyes got big. "Are you sure?"

Diggy wondered instantly if he'd fucked up, but said, "Of course I'm sure."

Sho's face lit up like Reddy the Kilowatt Man holding a bazillion-watt lightbulb while standing on the face of the sun. "That's good," he said. "Because we don't have enough currency to cover your change."

CHAPTER FORTY-FOUR

As Diggy slid into the booth, Swearengen said, "Don't be giving the help that kind of currency. You do that and they won't come to work anymore."

Stick scooted next to Diggy. Swearengen sat across from them.

"How much is one of them rooleys worth?" Diggy asked.

Swearengen grinned big, showing lots of big white teeth. "You don't know, do you?" He chuckled.

"Don't know what?"

Diggy looked at Stick, who just shrugged.

"I don't know," Diggy said. "I don't know shit about no rooleys."

"It's worth fifty thousand gerro," Swearengen said.

"*What the fuck?*" Diggy blurted. He turned and looked at the smiling bartender behind the bar. "You tellin' me I just gave forty-nine thousand gerro to the fuckin' bartender?"

"That's exactly what I'm telling you," Swearengen said, snorting and laughing so hard he doubled over the table.

Diggy, still staring at the bartender, said, "I'm gonna go get my money back."

Stick grabbed his arm. "You can't do that. You gave it to him. If you take it back now, you'll be an Indian giver."

Diggy relaxed a bit and looked at Stick. Then he looked down at Stick's hand on his shoulder. "Two things, Stick," he said. "One, you ain't supposed ta say Indian no more. It ain't proper. It's indigenous peoples, so I'd be an indigenous peoples giver."

"I don't think that's proper either," Stick said.

"Two," Diggy continued, "you better never put your grubby paws on my arm again, 'less you intend to lose 'em."

Stick grinned. "Same old Dig."

"Here's some advice," Swearengen said, looking at Diggy. "I don't know where the hell you got that rooley, but if you've got more of 'em, I'd keep them hidden away and keep your mouth shut about them. That kind of currency will get a man done up pretty bad here."

"In Hades, or in this bar?"

"Both."

Diggy raised an eyebrow. "That's fine," he said, "'cause that was the only one I had." Stick thought this was an obvious lie, but then considered perhaps it was only obvious to him because he knew Diggy as well as he knew the dick-beating palm of his own hand.

Diggy poured himself a drink. He looked at Stick, who was chewing his fingernails. "You got yourself tore up pretty bad. How the hell'd you manage that? You look like you done ran into Tina again."

Stick gave him the stink eye. Swearengen asked, "Who is this Tina?"

Diggy grinned. "What? Sticky ain't told you about Tina yet? I'm surprised, 'cause this fool is so in love with her he can't see straight."

"And I repeat, who the fuck is Tina?" Swearengen asked.

"She's my ex-wife," Stick said.

"She's a cold-hearted devil bitch is what she is," Diggy said.

Stick was going to argue this but found he couldn't, so he kept his mouth shut.

"So really," Diggy said, looking at Stick. "How'd you get all tore up like this?"

"Ballywonk," Swearengen said flatly.

Diggy looked at him, shaking his head. "Bally-*who*?"

"It's a big lizard," Stick explained. "About the size of a dog. All scaly and mean, with a long tail and great big sharp teeth. People apparently keep them as pets."

"I seen one of those," Diggy said. "Some fucker was walkin' it on a leash like a dog." He looked at Stick. "How'd you get attacked by one? What, you was just walkin' down the street mindin' your own business and a big fuckin' lizard jumped out and attacked you?"

"I was..." Stick started, but then looked at Swearengen. "It doesn't really matter. I was doing some work for Mr. Swearengen and the damn thing attacked me."

Diggy looked back and forth between the two men. "What kinda work you doin'?"

"We'll talk about it later," Stick said.

Swearengen raised his eyebrows and cocked his head. "Oh, will we now, Sticky boy?"

Stick met his gaze. "I was hoping we could bring him in."

"In on what?" Diggy asked.

Swearengen looked at Stick. "Is he tough?"

This caused Diggy to stop his line of questioning. Looking at Swearengen, he said, "You're goddamn right I'm tough."

Still looking at Stick, Swearengen asked, "He tougher than you?"

"He's good," Stick said.

"*Shiiiit!*" Diggy spat. He looked at Stick. "I'm way tougher than your no-fightin' ass."

Stick grinned and looked at Swearengen. "I'd say he's about the same as me."

"Like hell I am," Diggy protested. "It's like comparin' a mountain lion to a tabby cat."

Stick asked, "Who won the last time we fought?"

"That shit don't count," Diggy said. "Who won the time we fought before that?"

"I'd say it was a draw."

"Draw, my ass!"

"What's the deal with you two?" Swearengen asked. "You two fight an awful lot for your being friends."

"It ain't like that," Diggy said. "We just fuckin' around."

"Sibling rivalry," Stick said.

Swearengen looked at them, grinning, his eyes moving from one to the other. "Well, if you two are siblings, I hate to tell you fellas this, but your mama was doing a bit of outside fucking."

"You'd best not talk about Diggy's mama like that," Stick said. "He's gets really sensitive about her prowling around for white dick."

"You ain't funny," Diggy said.

"I'm the funniest guy you know."

"In your dreams. In your fuckin' dreams."

CHAPTER FORTY-FIVE

"So, what is it you do that you need employees?" Diggy asked.

"I know you guys haven't been here long," Swearengen said, "so I'm not sure where to start. Do you know about the system here in Hades, and the criminal hierarchy we've got?"

"No" Diggy said. "No one's told me about any of that."

"Most of the men in Hades are criminals and lowlifes, right?" Swearengen said.

Diggy nodded.

"Okay, so everyone here is involved in some type of criminal enterprise, be it drugs, robbery, politics—"

"*Politics?*" Diggy asked.

"You ever seen bigger criminals than those cocksuckers?"

Diggy rubbed his chin. "Nope. Not a one."

Swearengen spoke with his hands, which bounced around on the tabletop as he explained.

"Hades is made up of a million or so crime operations," Swearengen said. "Each operation has a boss."

"And you're one of them," Diggy guessed.

Swearengen nodded. "And I'm one of them. But I'm small potatoes compared to a lot of 'em. As I said, there's a hierarchy, a totem pole of importance, so to speak. There are three tiers of these organizations, each one holding greater significance."

"What's yours?" Diggy asked.

"I'm on the lower tier," Swearengen said. "I've got a crew of less than fifty men." He looked at Stick and then Diggy. "I've got Sticky boy here on the team, and I'd like to have you as well. I can tell by looking at you, the same as I could with Stick, that you're a tough bastard."

"How's that?"

"You've got scars around your eyes, but your nose hasn't been broken."

Diggy nodded. "Okay. Go on"

"There are three tiers, the top one being the most powerful. Then, above those, is Satan."

"*Satan?*" Diggy asked.

Swearengen nodded. "He and his minions oversee everything. As I was telling Stick earlier, there's no policing here as far as crime goes. The sky is the limit, as they say. There is some re-killing, but not as much as there was back home."

"Why's that?"

"Honor among thieves," Stick interjected.

Diggy looked at him, not understanding this piss-poor explanation.

"One thing he didn't tell you that you're gonna be interested in," Stick said, "is that Hitler is one of the top tier crime bosses."

"Not top tier," Swearengen said. "Second tier."

"*What, Hitler wasn't a bad enough man to be on the top tier?*" Diggy asked.

"It's not about that here," Swearengen said. "It's about paying dues and working your way up. Earning your place."

"And Hitler hasn't earned his place?" Stick asked.

"He's kind of a fuck up."

"But you're on the bottom tier," Diggy said. "So what does that make you?"

Swearengen grinned. "A man who knows exactly where he wants to be."

"If every boss is some important criminal from Earth's past, then who are you?" Diggy asked.

"No, no, that's not right," Swearengen said. "While I'm sure more than a few of the bosses held some significance back in the world, most of them are just regular men."

"Like you."

"Like me. I was a pimp back in Deadwood. I did a few other unseemly things, but mostly I was a pimp."

"I guess there ain't nobody to pimp here," Diggy said.

"You're wrong about that. We've got prostitutes, just not females."

"You still pimp?"

Swearengen shrugged. "I do a little bit of everything to keep my piece of the pie, and one of those things is pimping. As such, the gigolos stay on the second and third floors of the hotel upstairs, and my men maintain residences on the fourth and fifth."

"What about the cops? What are they like?"

"Nonexistent," Swearengen said. "There are no police here, but there are things that are policed. The things they police here are the creation of comforts, such as umbrellas, clothing, books, music—"

"There's no music?" Diggy asked.

"It's prohibited," Swearengen said. "You can hum, but that's it. You can't even sing to yourself."

"What happens if you do?"

"You get electrocuted, something like having lightning course through your body, for *days*," Swearengen said grimly. "What would probably be a week back home. It doesn't re-kill you, but you'd prefer dying. No man commits the same offense— or any offense, really—after experiencing that."

"Shit," Diggy said. "That sounds intense. But how do they know if you do one of those things, like, say, sing a song?"

"The controllers see everything," Stick said. "It's like if there were security cameras everywhere, only there aren't any. At least not that I've seen."

"No cameras," Swearengen said. "The bastards just *see*. They see everything, and they know everything."

"Huh," Diggy said, considering this. "And Satan runs all that?"

"He does," Swearengen said.

"What's Satan like?" Diggy asked. "Is he red with horns and all that?"

Swearengen chuckled. "No, he's just a man. I've never laid eyes on him myself, but they say he's a dapper cocksucker, very nicely dressed." He looked at Diggy. "Like you."

"Maybe *I'm* Satan," Diggy joked. "You ever think of that?"

"You're worse than Satan," Stick said.

"Fuck you, Stick." Diggy turned back to Swearengen. "What about God?"

"What about him?"

"Is he real?"

"I have no idea," Swearengen said. "No one here does. There are rumors, but that's about it. And you know how unreliable rumors are."

Wearing a big smile, he slid out of the booth and stood. "I've got business to attend to. It was nice meeting you, Mr. Diggs. I hope you'll come and work for us. Now, if you gentlemen will excuse me, I've got business to attend to, so I'll leave you to catch up."

CHAPTER FORTY-SIX

When Swearengen was back up at the bar, Diggy asked, "What do you *really* think about this guy?"

"I think he's on the level," Stick said.

"So you think we should work for him?"

"What else are we gonna do? Last I looked, we're in this shithole for the rest of eternity. Like Prince said, that's a mighty long time. Besides, we've got to do *something*. And if everyone's working for one organization or another, this one's as good as the next."

"But you don't *know* that," Diggy said. "There might be one out there fits us better."

"If we find something else down the road, we'll jump ship. There's nothing saying we've got to stay here forever. The pay is good, but then there's another thing."

"What's that?"

"He made me a deal."

"Swearengen?"

Stick looked at him like he was stupid. "Of course, Swearengen. Who the fuck else would I be talking about? Santa Claus?"

"With your dumb ass, it's hard to tell. It could be Santa Claus."

"Anyway," Stick said, ignoring this, "there's this guy called the Oracle."

"That's his name?"

"It's a title, I think. But the Oracle lets you go back to Earth—"

"*We get to go back to Earth?!*"

Stick held up the palm of his hand. "Slow down, Speed Racer. What I was going to say was, there's a way you can go back to Earth, but only for a short time."

"How short?"

"Swearengen said it's about an hour, give or take."

"Give or take?"

"He said it's different every time, but it's always close to that."

"So what's the deal?"

"He said if I work for him for a while, he'll let me go back," Stick said. "He promised he could make that happen."

Diggy raised an eyebrow. "Let me guess."

"What?"

"You gonna go back and talk to that bitch."

"What bitch?" Stick asked, knowing full well.

"What bitch? Tina bitch. How's that?"

"It's not like that, Dig."

"But that's your plan?"

"Well," Stick said weakly.

"You get the chance to go back for an hour and *that's* what you gonna do? You gonna go see the one person on the planet who don't wanna see you." Diggy shook his head. "I love you like a brother, Stick, but you a dumb motherfucker."

"It's not like that."

"Then what's it like?"

"I just want to try to make things right. End things on a good note. Get some closure."

Diggy threw his hands up, shaking his head. "She hates your ass, Stick. I know you don't wanna hear it, but she does. The only closure she wants to see is them closin' the lid on your casket. What you need to be doin' is goin' to see your son."

"Jim hates me, Dig. You know that."

"And Tina don't? Look, Stick, you got a better chance of makin' things right with him than you do with her. If you only get one chance, don't waste it on her. I know you love her, but you gotta let her go. Jimmy's still your son, Stick. He gon' always be family. He's your blood. Tina ain't blood."

Stick sat there looking down at the table for a long moment. Finally, he looked up at Diggy and said, "Anyway, I figure if you come to work for him, Swearengen might take you to see the Oracle too."

"That does sound good."

"What would you do if you went back?"

"That's a good question." Diggy considered this. "I guess I'd go see Alyssa." He leveled his gaze at Stick. "You know why? 'Cause she's my fuckin' daughter, Stick, and if you're a dad, that's what you do."

"It's not that I don't love Jim."

"But you love Tina more."

"Okay, fine," Stick said. "If you want to put it that way, then yeah. But it's not that I love her more. Not really."

"But?"

"She's the priority."

He could almost feel Diggy's judgmental stare burning into his flesh. He pointed at his friend. "You don't get to judge me."

"Like hell. Last I knew, it was a free country."

"We aren't in America anymore," Stick said. "We're in Hades, and it doesn't seem all that free to me."

CHAPTER FORTY-SEVEN

Diggy and Stick walked to the entrance of the bar so they could go for a stroll and talk some more. They were laughing and talking, lost in discussion, when a voice said, *"There you are, you black fucker! I been lookin' for you!"*

They turned to see a poorly dressed one-eyed man with bushy white eyebrows and an equally bushy white beard standing a few feet away, glaring at Diggy.

"You make friends everywhere you go, don't you?" Stick said.

Diggy pointed at the old man, and there was fire in his eyes. "Trust me when I say this—you don't want no part of what I got ta give. You done already got your ass whupped once. You lookin' for an encore?"

"I'll kill your ass!"

Neither Diggy nor Stick was moved by this. Stick turned to Diggy. "Who is this?"

Taking his jacket off, Diggy said, "He's just a guy I had to rob for his clothes."

"You're damn right you did!" the old man yelled.

Looking at Diggy's clean white suit, Stick said, "Well, they are pretty nice clothes."

Diggy handed the jacket to Stick. "Not these clothes. I stole these from another guy. This fucker here just had some tattered-ass hobo clothes."

"Jesus, Dig," Stick said. "How many men you steal clothes from?"

Diggy turned to face the old man. He raised his fists, ready to fight. "You a hundred and six years old, motherfucker. I bet you wasn't even shit when you was young. I really hate that you makin' me do this, old man. You sure you don't want out? You leave now, I'll let you go, ass-whuppin' free."

The old man didn't back down. "Screw you, you dumb fuck!" he said, raising his bony old man fists.

Diggy looked at Stick. "Some folks never learn."

Stick shrugged. "What can you do?"

Diggy moved confidently toward the old man, stepped forward with his right foot, and delivered a hard right to the old man's chin. The old man had been semi-blocking with his hands, but Diggy's punch had smashed its way through. Diggy felt the man's jaw shatter when he connected, and just like that, the old man went flying back onto the floor.

Diggy grinned and rubbed his knuckles. "I still got it."

Stick rolled his eyes and handed the suit back. "Because you knocked out Glass Joe? You could have fought a fucking chair and it would have put up more of a fight than this guy."

Seeing that his shirt had come untucked when he'd punched the man, Diggy made a sour face. "Look what this cockfucker did," he muttered. "I'm untucked." Diggy's face twisted in disapproval, and he angrily kicked the unconscious man.

CHAPTER FORTY-EIGHT

They were standing in the hall on the ninth floor of the hotel above the Gem. To be precise, they were standing in front of room 902. Stick handed Diggy the key and held his hand out toward the door, ushering him in.

"Here we are," Stick said.

Diggy took the key and stuck it into the lock. Diggy heard the lock click, and he pushed the door open. Diggy stood in the doorway for a moment, assessing the room.

"I didn't know it was furnished," Diggy said.

"It belonged to one of the guys I beat up when I got here," Stick said. "Mine did too."

"What guys?"

"It's a long story. I'll tell you about it later."

"What happened to 'em?" Diggy asked. "Where'd they go?"

Stick grinned. "Swearengen said he was so embarrassed by them getting their asses beat by one guy—"

"You?"

"Right," Stick said, nodding. "He was so embarrassed that he fired them on the spot."

"I can't say as I blame him. It's a bad look, two guys gettin' beat by your sorry ass."

"Tell me again who won the last time we fought," Stick said.

"I told you, that shit don't count."

"I'm tired of hearing that," Stick said. "Why do you say it

138

doesn't count?"

"You know damn well why it don't count."

"Why?"

"'Cause it was a Tuesday, and you know Tuesday's my bad luck day," Diggy said. "I don't fuck with Tuesdays."

Stick looked at Diggy. "How long have we been friends, Dig?"

"A long-ass time."

"Right," Stick said. "So why is it I'm just now hearing about your aversion to Tuesdays?"

"I've told you a couple times. But you don't listen. See, this is why Tina divorced your ass."

"Why do you say that?"

"Me and you, we're practically married," Diggy said. "And you don't listen. Never, ever, ever. You keep fuckin' around, I'm gonna divorce your ass too."

Stick sat down in the recliner by the window. "I should be so lucky."

"I don't feel appreciated."

"I got you this job, didn't I?"

"Yeah, I guess. But I ain't decided if it's a good job yet."

"Swearengen's been alright to me so far," Stick said. "But you never know."

"Benny was nice to us once upon a time too."

CHAPTER FORTY-NINE

The next day, or at least what he thought was the next day, Diggy sat with Stick and Swearengen in the same back booth as before. As Swearengen poured them all a drink, he looked across the table at Diggy.

"So, what's it going to be?" Swearengen asked. "Are you going to come and work for me, or not?"

Swearengen held out a glass for Diggy. Diggy met his gaze and took the glass.

"Stick told me about the Oracle," Diggy said.

Swearengen smiled. "I'm sure he did."

"He told me you said you'd set him up with the Oracle if he worked here for a while."

Swearengen nodded. "I like to give my men incentives to be here. I figure men like you could be working for any of these assholes. And the only asshole I want you working for is me. So, to keep you here, I like to provide extra incentives."

"On top of the money you'd pay us?" Diggy asked.

Swearengen nodded. "On top of the money."

"If I come to work for you, will you give me a go with the Oracle too?"

"Provided your work is on par with Sticky boy's," Swearengen said, "and Stick has assured me it will be, then yes, I'll take you to meet the Oracle for, what did you say? A *go*? Yes, I will most certainly do that for you, Mr. Diggy."

"No mister," Diggy said. "Just Diggy."

"Yeah, Dig's got a big enough head already," Stick said. "You go around calling him mister, and before long, he's going to get the idea he's something special."

Diggy said, "Motherfucker, I *am* somethin' special."

Diggy and Stick both laughed. Swearengen, not laughing, said, "How about it? Are you coming to work for me or not?"

"I'll work for you," Diggy said. "But we on a trial basis."

"Fair enough," Swearengen said. Then he raised his glass. "A toast!"

Diggy and Stick raised their glasses to touch his.

"To Diggy and Stick being part of the team!"

CHAPTER FIFTY

They were side by side, walking in the rain, each of them carrying a claw hammer at his side.

"I'll tell you one thing," Diggy said. "I'm tired of all this goddamn darkness. I miss daylight."

"I can almost live with the darkness. It's the fucking rain I'm tired of."

"Well, I'm tired of both."

"So am I," Stick said. "I didn't say I wasn't. I'm just saying I'm the *most* tired of the rain."

"You complainin' ain't gonna make it stop, you know."

"You think it ever stops raining?" Stick asked. "Maybe even once every hundred years?"

"I asked a fella that," Diggy said. "An old Korean dude who'd been here for a couple hundred years."

"What did he say?"

"He said he'd never seen it stop raining for even a minute the entire time he'd been here. He said when he'd asked men about it when he first got to Hades, they told him they'd never seen it stop raining either."

"Well, fuck," Stick muttered.

"You said a mouthful."

"You know what I wish?"

Diggy turned to look at him. "You best not say nothin' havin' to do with Tina, or so help me God, I will knock your fuckin' teeth out."

"No, not Tina," Stick said, slightly annoyed. "I was just gonna say I wished we had guns for this."

"Me too," Diggy said. "How we even supposed to scare this guy?"

"Here we are, Swearengen sending us out to rough up some unlucky bastard, and we've got to do it without a gun."

"The upside is that he ain't gon' have a gun neither."

Stick held up his hammer. "At least we've got these."

"They'll come in real handy if there's any nails need hammered," Diggy said dryly.

"I don't even know if they've got nails in Hades. I've never thought about it."

"They must have nails," Diggy reasoned. "Or else, why the hell they got hammers?"

"Maybe just for beating the shit out of people," Stick said. "That seems like a popular pastime here."

"We been workin' for Swearengen for a minute now. When's he gonna let us meet the Oracle, and when's he gon' find Dread Corbin?"

"Who gives a fuck about Dread Corbin?" Stick said. "We don't even have to kill him. It's not like Benny's ever going to know, and he couldn't touch us here even if he did."

"I'm gonna kill Corbin," Diggy said.

Stick looked at his partner. "Why?"

"'Cause I gave my word."

"That's it?"

"My word is my bond, Stick. Maybe that don't mean shit to you, but it means a hell of a lot to me. That's how my daddy raised me. He said a man's word is all he's really got in this world."

"Well, we're not in that world anymore, Dig. It's not important here."

"It's important to me," Diggy insisted. "If I make somebody a promise, I'm gonna do my best to keep it."

The two men continued walking toward the address Swearengen had given them. Neither spoke for a few blocks. Stick wasn't particularly good at letting silence hang in the air, never had been, but was aware of that fact and was now making a conscious effort. Although he was fairly proud of himself for having been quiet during this span, he was the one who broke the silence.

"How do you think the Oracle works?" Stick asked, throwing it out to spark conversation.

"How do I know?" Diggy said. "Do I look like a Oracle expert?"

"It's just a weird deal, and I've been trying to figure out how it might work."

"What have you come up with so far?"

"Nothing really," Stick admitted. "Since he sounds like some kind of mythical guy from one of those *Lord of the Rings* movies, I kind of see him as an old guy who looks like Gandalf, with a long white beard. As to how he sends you home, I figure maybe he sprinkles magic dust on you or something."

Diggy gave him a look of irritation.

"What?" Stick asked.

"*Magic dust?* That's what you come up with? You must be smokin' magic dust."

Still walking, Stick considered this.

"That didn't land right," he said.

"Whatchu mean?"

"Your joke. About the dust. I think it's one of those jokes that sounds good in your head, like it's gonna be funny, but then when you say it, it's not."

"What the hell do you know about comedy?" Diggy said. "You some kinda low-rent Seinfeld? The only time you ever funny is when you not tryin' ta be."

"This is the longest fucking walk," Stick complained. "It's like the Bataan Death March."

"A-hundred-and-some blocks?" Diggy said. "This is some

bullshit. What they need here even more than they need guns is cars. Man, what I wouldn't give for a car right now. It ain't even gotta be a nice car, it could be a fuckin' hooptie. Just *somethin'*, cause this walkin' sucks donkey dicks."

"I don't know exactly how far this is," Stick said, "but a hundred and seven blocks is at least—at the *very* least—ten miles."

"That's a long way," Diggy said, sounding tired. "Especially in this rain. By the time we get there, we gon' be too tired to kick this dude's ass."

CHAPTER FIFTY-ONE

When they lost count of the number of blocks they'd walked, they decided to stop for a drink. In Hades, there was a bar on almost every block. The bar they stopped at was a rundown hole-in-the-wall called Smokey's Place. Judging from the two men standing outside, Stick figured it was going to be a black bar.

"Come on," Diggy said. "Let's get a drink."

Stick was a tough man, but truth be told, he was a tad bit nervous.

"There don't seem to be any white people here."

"Sounds good to me," Diggy said. "I feel like I already got one too many white dudes to deal with."

"Really, though, what if they don't want me here?"

Diggy grinned. "I was you, I'd keep 'hold 'a that hammer."

"Thanks for the encouragement, Dig."

"Don't mention it. It's the least I can do."

"The *very* least," Stick said.

Diggy nodded at the man standing closest to the door, and the man nodded back. Stick looked at him and said, "How's it going?" but the man just stared at him.

"Friendly fucker," Stick said.

A bell rang as Diggy pushed the door open. He stepped inside with Stick behind.

There was a smattering of clientele, all black. A couple guys looked up at first, and soon everyone in the place was looking at Stick.

The fat-but-fairly-tough-looking bartender shook his head.

"Uh-uh," he said. "This ain't that kinda place."

Diggy met the bartender's gaze. "Oh yeah? What kinda place is it?"

"The kinda place that don't cater to guys like him."

Diggy looked at Stick, grinning as he did. "What is you, Stick? About six-four?" He looked back at the bartender, nodding. "I get it. You sayin' you don't cater to dudes that's six-four, right? I get it, man. They can be a real pain in the ass. Lemme tell ya, this motherfucker here—"

"We don't serve crackers," the bartender said.

"It's a good thing we didn't bring any cheese then," Diggy said.

The tension in the room was thick enough to cut with a knife. Stick would have been just fine with leaving, but Diggy was in full Diggy mode.

"You ain't funny," the bartender said.

Stick grinned and looked at Diggy. "See? I keep trying to tell him that, but he doesn't listen."

No one laughed, grinned, smiled, or smirked. A few of the bar's patrons were starting to rise from their seats.

"You better get your asses outta here," the bartender said.

"Or what?" Diggy asked.

"Whatchu think?"

Diggy looked him over. "I think you're a sorry-ass mama's boy. That's what I think. I think you probably died back home doin' somethin' stupid, and I think if you keep pushin' this, we 'bout to see a repeat."

Diggy made a point to let him see the hammer, holding it in front of his body, resting its head in the palm of his other hand. This didn't go unnoticed by the bartender.

"I don't know who the fuck you think you are," the bartender said, "but there's about thirty brothers in here who would be more than happy to stomp a mud hole in both your asses."

"Thirty against two," Stick said. "What do you think of those odds?"

"Sounds good to me." Diggy looked at the bartender. "I think you better fix us that drink now."

The bartender stood there staring at him, and Diggy could see the wheels in his head turning. Then, finally, the man's shoulders slumped a little.

"Tell you what," the bartender said. "I'ma fix you one drink. One. Uno, motherfucker. *One.* You two drink that shit with the quickness and get the fuck out."

Diggy grinned. "Don't mind if I do."

Diggy and Stick both sat at the bar. They could see everyone in the place, so if anyone tried any silly shit, they would see it coming.

Every eye in the place remained on them.

"It's kind of different doing this shit without any music playing," Stick said. "Kind of heightens the tension."

Diggy nodded. "I knew somethin' was different, but I didn't know what. But you right, it's a whole 'nother vibe."

The bartender set two shot glasses in front of them. He poured the whiskey and looked at Diggy. "You got some big balls, you know that?"

Diggy smiled. "Don't I know it. And lemme tell ya, it's hard got-damn work luggin' these heavy fuckers around."

CHAPTER FIFTY-TWO

"You could have got us killed back there," Stick said.

"But I didn't."

"But you could have."

"Lots of things could have happened that didn't," Diggy said. "Your daddy coulda done the world a favor and wore a damn rubber, but he didn't. Tina coulda stayed with your sorry ass, but she didn't."

"That's kind of harsh, don't you think?"

Diggy looked at him and shrugged. "It *was* harsh, but it was her that did the shit, not me."

"Why you always gotta say that shit about her?"

"Because your ass don't. I'm just tryin' to remind you what that bitch did."

"I know she left me," Stick said. "I don't need you to remind me."

Diggy gave him some serious side-eye. "Not only did she leave your ass, but she left you to fuck the dude who got our badges taken away. If that ain't a great big 'fuck you,' then I don't know what is."

"It was pretty much a 'fuck you' from life," Stick said.

Diggy stopped and wheeled around, looking at him. "Shit, man. It wasn't life that climbed into bed and started fuckin' Keeling. Wasn't nobody else but Tina's ass. Just her and her alone. Nobody, I repeat *no-body*, made her do any of that. You say you were a shitty husband. Yeah, you were a bad husband, but there's ways to fix that shit. Marriage counseling and whatever, but you don't go behind a man's back and start fuckin' his mortal enemy!"

They started walking again, and Stick asked, "You think Keeling is our mortal enemy?"

"You damn right he is."

"I dunno," Stick said. "I kind of think Benny owns that distinction, considering he made us kill ourselves and go to Hell."

"Hades," Diggy corrected. "But I suppose there's lots 'a guys could be our mortal enemy. We got a lotta enemies."

"Tina always said I was the kind of guy you either loved or hated."

"Nah, that's not true," Diggy said. "They just hate your ass." He paused for a moment. "You know, you just proved what I been sayin'. Tina said you was somebody you either love or hate. If she don't love you, then what the fuck does that tell you?"

"I think she still loves me on some level," Stick said.

Diggy chuckled. "Ain't no level to it, but you keep tellin' yourself that. Whatever helps you sleep."

Stick changed the subject. "You know what I think?"

"No, but I'm sure you gon' tell me."

"I think you went into that bar just to start shit."

A big, wise-ass grin appeared on Diggy's face. "You don't know me as well as you think you do."

"Bullshit, Dig," Stick said. "I know you about as well as anyone knows anybody else, and I believe with every fiber of my being that you went in there with the intention of starting shit."

Diggy shrugged. "What can I say? I got a lotta pent-up anger, and I gotta direct it someplace."

CHAPTER FIFTY-THREE

After sitting inside an entrance way and taking a breather, Diggy and Stick strode into the bodega where the man was supposed to be. There was a cluster of middle-aged Russians congregated inside the tiny store. Five in all. One was wearing old-time Western garb with a brown cowboy hat, duster, and gaudy, bright red cowboy boots.

"We're here to talk to Belochkin," Stick announced.

The men stood there for a moment, sizing them up.

"They're carrying hammers," one observed.

Red Boots asked, "What do you need?"

"You Belochkin?" Diggy asked.

"No."

"Why are you dressed like a cowboy?" Stick asked.

Diggy looked at him. "That ain't why we here."

Stick shrugged. "But I gotta know."

"I watch American cowboys on TV as young boy in Soviet Russia," Red Boots said. "Now I am cowboy."

Stick nodded. "Huh. Okay."

Diggy pointed at the men with his hammer. "Which of you fuckers is Belochkin?"

At that moment, a door closed in the back of the room.

"That is Belochkin," one of the men said, pointing toward the closed door.

"Christ," Diggy muttered.

"Are you guys his bodyguards?" Stick asked.

This caused a couple of the Russians to chuckle.

"We are not bodyguards," one said.

"We're just here for Belochkin," Diggy said. "Anyone don't want his ass cracked best hit the bricks."

"What does this mean, this ass cracked bricks hitting?" asked Red Boots.

"It means we're gonna beat the ever-livin' dog shit outta you if you don't get outta here right now," Diggy said.

And just like that, the men were all moving, on their way to the entrance.

"That door back there," Stick said. "Does it have an exit?"

"No," one of the men said. "Is supply closet."

"Have fun with Belochkin," another said as they were exiting. "He is what you call...*asshole.*"

"It'll be okay," Stick said, nodding toward Diggy. "I'm used to this guy, and he's an asshole if there ever was one."

Diggy gave him a tired look. "Hardy fuckin' har-har."

Diggy led the way up the narrow aisle to the closed door.

"Hey, guys," came a voice from behind.

They turned around to see that one of the men had returned.

"What's up?" Stick asked.

The man pointed toward a shelf filled with cigarette cartons behind the counter. They were all the same kind as there was only one kind of cigarettes in Hades.

"Can I take some cigarettes?" asked the man. "Pretty please and salt on top."

Diggy and Stick looked at each other like, *can you believe this shit?*

Diggy sighed. "Go ahead. Grab a couple and go."

Stick gave him a look, and Diggy shrugged.

The Russian was behind the counter, pulling down several cartons of cigarettes, one at a time, and tucking them under his arm.

"Christ, how many are you going to take?" Stick asked.

Growing impatient, Diggy said, "Just take what you got and go."

The man looked at him, blinked, took a step forward, then grabbed one last carton.

"What the fuck?" Diggy said. "You just had to take one more, didn't you?"

The man came around the counter carrying an ungodly number of cartons, all of which looked like they could fall out of his arms any second.

"No," Stick said sternly.

The man looked at him blankly, saying nothing.

"He told you to take what you had," Stick said. "But you had to go and grab another one."

The man just stared at him.

"Put one back," Stick commanded.

"Just one?" the man asked.

Diggy growled, "Man, will you just drop one on the floor and get your ass out?"

The man nodded and let a single carton slide out from under his arm and fall to the floor. Then he started toward the exit. As he was leaving, Stick said, "Thank you for shopping with us. Please come again."

CHAPTER FIFTY-FOUR

Diggy banged on the door.

"Bring your ass out here, Belochkin!"

"Why?" a voice inside the closet asked. "Why you want Belochkin?"

"We want to talk to you," Stick said.

"You want to kill Belochkin," said the frightened voice.

"No," Diggy said. "We just supposed to throw you a beatin'."

He tapped on the door with the head of the hammer.

"Come on, Belochkin," Diggy said. "You're makin' all this worse by stretchin' it out."

"Who send you to beat on Belochkin?" the man asked.

"We're not telling you until you come out," Stick said.

"Was it Popov?" asked the man. "Did Popov send you?"

"No," Diggy said. "It wasn't no Popov."

"How about Karev? Did Karev send you?"

"Nope, not Karev," Stick said. "Try again."

"Then Abelman, the Jew?"

Diggy and Stick looked at each other incredulously.

"This motherfucker got more enemies than we do," Diggy said.

"If you're not coming out, we're going to bust this door open," Stick said.

"If we have to do that, we fuckin' you up worse," Diggy said.

154

"Belochkin not come out," said the voice.

Diggy sighed and his shoulders relaxed. "Why's it always gotta be some bullshit?"

"Move out of the way," Stick said. "I'll kick the door in."

Diggy looked at him. "Why's it gotta be you?"

"We both know I'm better at it than you are."

Diggy shrugged. "Yeah, you right."

He stepped aside, and Stick stood in front of the door, squaring himself. He handed Diggy his hammer. "Take this for a minute, would you?" Stick resumed his stance. Under his breath, he counted: "one, two...three." When he reached three, Stick kicked the door with all the force he could muster. The door shot open, hitting Belochkin, who peeked around it with big eyes.

"You really not going to kill Belochkin?" the man asked.

"We just gon' teach you a lesson," Diggy said.

"And just so you know, it was Al Swearengen who sent us," Stick added.

Belochkin looked at them with tears in his eyes. "Okay," he said. "You may now beat on Belochkin."

CHAPTER FIFTY-FIVE

Diggy and Stick were making their way back to the Gem. They were walking the same way they'd come, only this time they were even more tired, and they were both carrying armfuls of cigarette cartons.

The rain was in their eyes and they were talking, as usual.

"I kinda hated to hear his bones break like that," Diggy said.

"I get that," Stick said, "but that's the job. Think of it this way, at least in Hades, broken bones fix themselves in a couple of hours."

"Still, it had to have hurt somethin' fierce."

"Hence the man's screams," Stick said.

"At least we didn't have to re-kill him."

"That's true, but you know, when I re-killed that guy for Swearengen—the bald fucker I told you about—I didn't feel all that bad."

"Why's that?"

"Because he was already dead," Stick said. "All I was doing was *re*-killing him, so I figure it's not as bad as killing somebody back home."

"I gotta disagree with you there."

"How so?"

"Because when you re-kill somebody here, they go on to someplace that's even worse than this," Diggy said.

"We don't know that as a fact," Stick said.

"But that's what everybody says, and it seems right. They ain't gonna just let you die and escape this shit, or every motherfucker here would be gettin' hisself re-killed."

Stick considered this and decided Diggy was right.

"I've got a weird question," Stick said.

"Big surprise," Diggy said. "Everything comes out your mouth is weird."

Stick ignored this. "Two of those Russians were toothless."

"So? What about it?"

"I've seen a lot of guys with no teeth here," Stick said. "Doesn't that seem kind of strange to you?"

"Nah, I know why they ain't got no teeth."

"Why's that?"

"I was talkin' to that old Korean dude I was tellin' you about, and he said that you come here exactly the way your body was before you died."

Stick nodded. "That's why a lot of these guys are old. They're the same age they were when they died."

"Right," Diggy said. "But he also said that people who had prosthetic devices—things like canes, hearing aids, glasses, wheelchairs—are just shit outta luck. They ain't got none of that shit here."

"Ahh, I get it. The guys without teeth don't have their dentures."

"Bingo."

"This leads me to another question, though. Where are the people without their wheelchairs? I haven't seen any—"

"I think we got a problem," Diggy interrupted.

Hearing the alarm in his voice, Stick looked where Diggy was staring, seeing a group of husky, bearded thirty-somethings dressed like Vikings on the corner under the streetlight ahead. And they were staring back.

"You think those are real Vikings?" Stick asked.

"How the fuck do I know? The only Viking I know is Randy Moss."

"Maybe we could just cross the street and they won't fuck with us."

At that moment, the band of Vikings started moving toward them.

CHAPTER FIFTY-SIX

As the Vikings grew nearer—they were about twenty feet away now—Diggy and Stick could see them eyeballing the cigarette cartons.

"What can we do for you fellas?" Stick asked.

Diggy remained silent, putting on his meanest face.

The Viking leading the pack—it was instantly apparent he was their leader—raised his arm and pointed toward the cigarettes.

"Give us your cigarettes and we might allow you to pass," the Viking said.

Stick was about to agree and hand over the smokes, but Diggy spoke up. "You ain't getting' my fuckin' cigarettes."

Stick looked at him. *"Diggy."*

"Nah, man, I'm serious as a preacher," Diggy said. "These motherfuckers ain't gettin' my cigarettes."

"Who cares about the cigarettes?" Stick asked, flustered. "Cigarettes aren't worth getting re-killed over."

The Vikings watched this exchange.

"It's the principle of the matter," Diggy said. "These cigarettes are mine, and what's mine is mine. So I ain't givin' up these fuckin' cigarettes."

Stick did a slight shrug and turned to face the Viking leader.

"I guess you heard him," Stick said. "You can't have the cigarettes. You'll have to get your own."

"Then we will pummel you and take them."

Stick sighed.

Diggy and Stick dropped all the cartons simultaneously, both men squaring their feet in preparation for a fight.

Diggy flicked the end of his nose with his thumb.

"Come and get it, you chickenshits," he said.

Almost instantly, the men came rushing at them. There were eight of them. They were big, brawny fuckers, but they weren't great fighters. And they were slow; Diggy and Stick were both quicker than any of them.

One of the Vikings lowered his head as he ran at Stick, hoping to spear him with the horns atop his metal helmet. Stick thought the man was moving in slow motion, and he moved out of his way, easily avoiding him. When the momentum carried the man past Stick, Stick threw a hard punch into his back, catching him off guard. Stick threw himself toward the Viking, delivering three hard uppercuts into his spine, and the Viking fell onto the slick pavement. Stick then moved on him, kicking the Viking's face like he was kicking a field goal, and the Viking flopped back unconscious.

There wasn't time for Stick to admire his handiwork as another Viking blindsided him, crashing into him from behind. This sent Stick falling face-first onto the unconscious Viking he'd kicked. Somewhere between the collision and Stick's landing atop the unconscious man, he realized what was happening and made the necessary corrections. When his body struck the fallen Viking's body, Stick used the momentum to roll over so he was facing up, just in time to see his attacker diving at him. Just as the Viking landed on Stick, Stick kneed him hard in the groin. The Viking let out a pained groan, and Stick brought his right elbow up hard, knocking the man's head back. In a single fluid motion, Stick did this and pushed the Viking off him. The Viking was holding his body up with one arm, and Stick climbed on top of him, striking him with a flurry of punches, working his way up. The first punch struck the Viking's throat, causing him to lose his wind and bearings. The second punch struck the Viking's chin, rocking his head back against the pavement. The third blow struck the Viking's mouth, breaking his teeth, and the fourth and fifth smashed his nose, the fifth sending a sharp bone fragment into his brain, re-killing him instantly.

A few feet away, Diggy was fending off Vikings too. Having already knocked one of the bastards unconscious with a single punch to the cheek, he was now on top of another, smashing his fists hard against the Viking's face.

In the end, the Vikings gained the upper hand against both Diggy and Stick in the same way; while Diggy and Stick were on the ground, on top of Vikings, beating them, pairs of the bastards attacked them from behind. Diggy and Stick continued fighting with all the strength and ferocity they possessed, but to no avail.

CHAPTER FIFTY-SEVEN

Diggy felt a warm, scratchy tickle on his cheek. He smiled and opened his eyes. When he did, he saw the face of a reptile there, up close, its skinny, scratchy tongue flicking his face.

"*Arrrgggghhhh!*" he screamed, scooting himself back on the pavement. He saw what was licking him now—*a ballywonk!* Luckily, Diggy's abrupt screaming had startled the creature, and it scurried away. When Diggy had scooted himself back, he scooted into his still-unconscious friend.

"What the hell are you yelling about?" Stick asked groggily, squinting his eyes open to face the falling rain.

"I woke up and there was one of them ballywhoos lickin' my fuckin' face," Diggy said. He used his sleeve to wipe the spit off his cheek. His face was still wet with rain, but it was ballywonk saliva free.

Both men worked to push themselves up from where they'd been lying unconscious since being beaten and knocked out.

"Where are we?" Stick asked.

Diggy was rubbing his head. "I feel like I got hit by a freight train."

Then they remembered.

"It was those damned Vikings," Stick muttered.

"Fuckin' peckerheads musta knocked us out."

Diggy noticed something else. Looking down at his wet feet, which somehow felt even wetter than the rest of his body, he saw that the nice reptile shoes he'd stolen from the rich man were gone. There were only socks on his feet.

"*Jesus fuck!*" Diggy said.

"What? What is it?"

"My shoes. Them sons of fuck Viking dickshits stole my fuckin' shoes!"

Looking at Diggy's socked feet, Stick said, "You stole them first."

"That ain't the point," Diggy said. "It's the principle of the thing. You don't steal a man's shoes."

"But *you* stole them, Dig. You did the exact same thing."

"Fuck you, Stick."

Scanning the dark, wet pavement surrounding them, Stick said, "Those Viking pricks took all the cigarettes too."

CHAPTER FIFTY-EIGHT

They were walking in the rainy darkness, and Stick and Diggy were discussing the way serious injuries healed themselves in Hades.

"How about severed limbs?" Diggy asked. "Like, if I chopped off one of them Viking bastards' arms, would it grow back?"

"I don't think so."

"Why's that?"

"Because when Swearengen was telling me about it, he didn't say anything like that," Stick said.

"There's a lotta dumb shit here that don't make no sense."

"Like what?"

"Like *every-goddamn-thing*," Diggy said. "Like the fact that you gotta steal clothes just to keep from walkin' around with your jimmy danglin'. That's some fucked up shit. Or the fact that all they have to drink is whiskey."

"How the hell is whiskey a punishment anyway?" Stick said. "That seems like a reward."

"Same thing with cigarettes."

"Although, to be fair, the cigarettes taste awful."

"That's true," Diggy said, nodding. "Worse than generic cigarettes back home. The damn things taste like ass."

"I hate it here," Stick said.

Diggy nodded. "Me too. I wanna go home."

They walked a little further and Diggy said with a half-smirk,

"I'll bet you ain't no atheist now."

Stick looked at him blankly. "What do you mean?"

"We're in the afterlife," Diggy said. "If that ain't proof that God's real, I don't know what is."

Stick considered this. "I don't know," he said. "It doesn't really prove anything. No one here knows for sure whether God is real or not, so how's that any different?"

Diggy stopped and looked at his friend with big, angry eyes. *"How's it different?* Are you outta your rabbit-ass mind? For starters, we're dead, man, and yet here we are! That's pretty significant, wouldn't you say? Then, on top of that, Satan is here. *Motherfuckin' Satan!* He's literally a dude just walkin' around here somewhere."

"He's got a car," Stick reminded him.

"But he's here!"

Stick stared at him. "Have you *seen* Satan? I mean *you,* personally, have you seen him?"

Diggy made a clucking sound with his teeth. "Just cause I ain't seen him don't mean he ain't real!"

"That's the same thing you said about God," Stick said. "And we still don't know. So no, Dig, nothing's changed. I'm still an atheist. Until somebody proves otherwise, I'll remain an atheist."

Diggy looked around incredulously. "Where the fuck do you think we are, Stick?"

Stick nodded. "I know, I know. It's supposed to be Hell, but what if it's not? What if this is like that *Twilight Zone* episode where the guy thinks he's in Hell but then finds out he's actually on another planet?"

"Goddammit, Stick," Diggy muttered. "There ain't no episode of *The Twilight Zone* like that. You just made that shit up."

"How do you know?"

Diggy stared at him. "'Cause I done seen all one hundred fifty-six episodes of *The Twilight Zone,* and that ain't one of 'em!"

"Maybe it's an *Outer Limits* then. Or *One Step Beyond.*"

"It ain't no *Outer Limits* nor none of 'em. But that don't matter right now. What matters is that my partner, my road dog, my ace boon, believes we might actually be prisoners of aliens someplace in outer space."

Stick shrugged. "I can't rule it out."

Diggy turned and looked into his eyes. "So you can't believe in God because you don't know for a fact he exists, but you *can* believe that we're somewhere in space?"

"I didn't say that was the truth. I just said I can't rule it out."

Diggy turned away in disgust. "You a dumb motherfucker, Stick."

CHAPTER FIFTY-NINE

Diggy approached several men, trying to find someone wearing shoes that might fit him. Once he located a man with the adequate footwear—a Puerto Rican wearing brown slip-ons—Diggy and Stick rolled him, knocked him out, and took the shoes.

"These don't fit too good," Diggy complained about two minutes later.

"*What?!*"

"They're half a size too big."

CHAPTER SIXTY

They were sitting in Swearengen's booth, waiting for him to make an appearance. Diggy and Stick were a common sight at Swearengen's table, and these days, they sat there more than anyone else, aside from Swearengen himself. They were sopping wet.

"There's water running down my ass crack," Stick said. "Do you think a guy ever *really* gets used to the rain?"

Diggy finished lighting his cigarette before answering. "I don't see how you could. I suppose, eventually, you learn to tolerate it. Sorta like havin' herpes."

Stick's eyes narrowed. "Is there something you haven't told me, Dig?"

Normally Diggy would become animated responding to such a smartass remark, but he was too tired to mess with it today. "My cousin, Melvin, had that shit. Up until then, I didn't know herpes was one that never went away. I thought maybe it was like the clap or somethin'."

"Melvin got used to it?"

"There's the distinction. He didn't get used to it, he *tolerated* it. Toleratin' is a whole other thing."

"Sort of like how I tolerate you," Stick said.

The two of them sat for a long while—what felt like two or three hours—wearily exchanging barbs and witticisms, until Swearengen finally made his entrance from the stairs across the room. Diggy and Stick often waited for Swearengen, but in Hades, everyone waited for everything because there were no clocks and no way to properly gauge the passing of time. This was especially confusing since it was always nighttime. As such, one man's waking day overlapped with the next man's sleeping night. It confused the hell out of Diggy and Stick, but Swearengen had assured them they would eventually get used to it. Or, as Diggy had said, *tolerate* it. When Stick had asked Swearengen how long it took him to grow accustomed to the day/night/time issue, he chuckled and said, "Only about fifty years. You're almost there!"

Swearengen first went to the bar to converse with Teddy, the guy who kept bar when Sho was asleep. They talked for a few minutes. Swearengen then looked at Diggy and Stick, noticing them for the first time. He lit up, smiled, grabbed another bottle and a glass, and headed toward them.

When he reached the table, he stood over them. "How'd it go with our dear friend, Mr. Belochkin?"

"Everything went fine," Diggy said.

Swearengen grinned and slid into the booth beside Stick. "Why do you both have black eyes and busted lips? Did Belochkin do that?"

"Wasn't nothin' like that," Diggy said.

"We got jumped coming back," Stick said.

Swearengen's eyes got big. "You got jumped? By *who*?"

"A bunch of fuckin' assholes is who," Diggy said.

"They looked like Vikings," Stick said.

A look of recognition washed over Swearengen's face, and he nodded in understanding. "Oh, yes, our Norwegian friends. They've become quite a nuisance."

"You know about them?" Diggy asked.

"Everyone does," Swearengen said. "They're a goddamn pain in the ass."

"They're one of the crime organizations?" Stick asked.

"Not really," Swearengen said. "They're rogues. More like

169

hoodlums. They're connected with Ronald Reagan's crew, the Brotherhood of Knives, but they're mostly independent."

"Wait," Diggy said. "Did you say *Ronald Reagan?*"

"Yeah," Stick said, *"Ronald Reagan is here?"*

"He runs a crew a couple hundred blocks away," Swearengen said.

"He was the president of the United States, you know," Stick said.

Swearengen nodded. "So I've heard. I met the man a couple of times. Nice enough fella."

"Why is he here?" Diggy asked.

Swearengen smiled. "All the presidents are here. I suspect they have to do a lot of really nasty shit behind closed doors." He opened his hands atop the table. "Heavy is the crown, etcetera, etcetera, et-fucking-cetera. But let's get back to our dear Mr. Belochkin. Did you have any problems handling him?"

"No," Stick said. "His bones broke easily enough."

Swearengen laughed a hearty laugh. "You broke a fair number of them?"

"Ol' Belochkin's got more broken bones than Evel Knievel," Diggy said.

Swearengen stopped laughing and looked at him with a confused expression. *"Evil who?"*

Stick put his arm around Swearengen. "Don't worry about it. He was a guy that lived on Earth a long time after you."

"Was he another president?"

"Nah," Diggy said. "Just some dude who liked jumpin' over shit with a motorcycle."

Swearengen looked even more confused now. *"Motorcycle?"*

Diggy and Stick looked at one another and laughed.

Swearengen poured each of them another drink, raising his.

"To what shall we toast?" Swearengen asked.

"How about Dread Corbin?" Diggy said.

Swearengen winked at him. "Why don't we toast to the

busted-to-shit Mr. Belochkin, shall we? Then, after that, we'll discuss your Mr. Corbin."

CHAPTER SIXTY-ONE

"Have you found him?" Stick asked.

"Not yet," Swearengen said. "But I'm looking. I'm extremely tied in to most of the shit that goes on around here, so I'll find the cocksucker. It's just matter of when."

Stick poured them each another glass.

"I have a question, though," Swearengen said. "There's something I don't quite understand."

"Okay," Diggy said.

"Stick has told me about how you two died—about the bastard who sent you here—"

"Benny Cordella," Diggy interjected.

Without skipping a beat, Swearengen continued. "And he's told me about your search for vengeance against this Dread Corbin. What I don't understand is, why follow through with it? Now that you're here, this Benny cocksucker can no longer hurt you. So, my question is, why follow through? Why do you care if this man did the other man wrong?"

Stick looked at Diggy. "You tell him, Dig. Tell him why we're going after him."

Diggy lowered his head slightly, looking back and forth between the men, prepared to meet resistance. "I gave my word," Diggy said. "And where I grew up, that's important. Not only is it important, but it's the *most* important thing. Your word is your bond, and if your word isn't worth a damn, then *you* ain't worth a damn."

"So?" Swearengen asked, staring at him blankly.

Diggy patted his chest. "I'm worth a damn."

Swearengen rubbed his mustache as he stared at Diggy, pondering his statement. "I'm not sure I agree with your logic, my friend."

"Join the club," Stick said.

"Truth of the matter is," Diggy said, "I don't give a blue fuck if either one of you agrees or understands. The only thing that matters to me is what *I* believe."

Swearengen stared at him, a half grin appearing on his face. "And you believe Dread Corbin should die."

Diggy nodded. "Deader than Bin Laden."

Swearengen downed another glass of the whiskey. "Well," he said, sounding tired, "I don't know who that is. But either way, agree with you or not, I'm going to locate Mr. Corbin for you." He stared at Diggy for a moment, considering this. "Once you fellas find him, how long do you expect you'll be gone?"

Diggy shrugged. "I guess it depends on where he's at and how long it takes for us to get there and back."

Stick said, "It shouldn't take long."

"Fair enough," Swearengen said. He turned toward Stick. "While I don't currently have the whereabouts of Dread Corbin, I do have a different form of compensation for you."

"What's that?" Diggy asked.

"This one is just for Stick," Swearengen said. "I promised him if he worked for me for a while, I'd take him to see the Oracle."

"What about me?" Diggy asked indignantly. "Don't I get to see him?"

Swearengen grinned and held the palm of his hand out toward Diggy. "Whoa! Hold your horses. Of course I'll take you to see the Oracle, but all in due time." He looked back at Stick. "Sticky boy has been working for me longer than you have. So for now, it's just going to be him. But I promise you, you work for me just a little longer, I'll see to it that you see the Oracle as well."

"I guess that works," Diggy said. "I haven't even decided who I'm gonna go see when I go back."

"I figured you'd see your daughter," Stick said.

Diggy glared at him. "And I figured you'd go see your son, so maybe we're both wrong."

Stick just nodded, looking wounded, and went back to his drink.

"I can't decide if I'm going to see my daddy or my daughter," Diggy said. "I love my daddy dearly, but I'm leanin' toward Alyssa. I spent a lot of time with my daddy, but I..." He choked up, but he steeled himself and pushed the sentiment back down. "I shoulda spent more time with her. And I'd like to say goodbye."

"Perhaps you'll see your father here in Hades one day soon," Swearengen said.

Diggy shot him a look that was equal parts shock and anger. "No, not my daddy. He ain't that type 'a man. He's a *good* man." He looked at Stick. "He ain't like us."

CHAPTER SIXTY-TWO

Swearengen gave Stick an address and told him the password was "Simon Says." The address was the location where he'd find the Oracle. "A man who goes by the name of 'Horsecock' will answer the door," Swearengen had told him. "Tell him the password and he'll let you in." Stick had then asked Swearengen why the man's name was Horsecock, to which Swearengen had given him a look and said, "Why the fuck do you think?" It was a stupid question and Stick was pissed at himself for having asked it.

The only bad part of all this was that the building was ninety-three blocks away, in the same direction he and Diggy had walked to visit Belochkin. This, of course, meant there was a good chance he would encounter the horde of Vikings again.

Stick had asked Swearengen if Diggy could accompany him on the trip, to which Swearengen had said yes, as long as Diggy waited outside. Realizing the probability that they would encounter the Vikings again, the two men armed themselves with weapons this time.

Stick had a machete. Diggy a hatchet.

CHAPTER SIXTY-THREE

The journey was an arduous one, the two men walking through the endless rain and darkness.

As they walked, Diggy said, "I really wish you wouldn't waste your trip with the Oracle to see Tina. You're wasting the opportunity. If you never take another piece of advice from me ever again, take this one, Stick."

Turning it over in his head, Stick said, "You think I should go talk to Jimmy."

Diggy nodded. "I do, but you could see anybody—*literally anybody*—and it would be better than going to see that bitch."

"Anybody?"

"Anybody."

"What if I went to see your mama?" Stick joked.

Diggy looked at him and shrugged. "My mama's dead, so fuck you for that, Mr. Funny Fuck, but I'd rather you see her than Tina's sorry ass."

"Why do always say that stuff about her?"

Diggy stopped and wheeled around to look at his partner. "Are you kiddin' me? Are you fucking kiddin' me? Tell me you're playin', please, Stick. You may or may not remember, but I was the one who sat with your ass after she left and you was thinkin' 'bout killin' yourself. I was the one who sat with your ass while you was drunk and cryin', talkin' about how nobody loved you."

This embarrassed Stick. "Look, man—"

"Ain't no 'look, man' to it," Diggy said with big, angry eyes. "I don't like her cause she fucked you up. And she *keeps* fuckin' you up. I used to hate her for it, but I can't anymore. You know why?"

"Come on, Dig."

"Do you know why?"

"Why?"

"'Cause it's *your* fault," Diggy said. "It's your goddamn fault, man. You're your own worst enemy. You can't leave well enough alone. You just keep runnin' back to get hurt, over and over. She done told you she didn't want you, but you don't learn. You never learn, Stick. Never. She don't want you, but you just keep doin' this shit."

Both of them were standing in the rain, facing each other. Stick looked down at the pavement.

"I don't want you to use your trip home to see her because she's gonna fuck you up again," Diggy said. "She will. You know goddamn well she will. And then what? Huh? Then what?"

Stick raised his head and stared at him, saying nothing.

"I'll fuckin' tell you what," Diggy said. "I'll be there with you, listenin' to you cry your fuckin' eyes out again." Completely angry now, Diggy turned away from Stick and threw his hands up. *"Jesus Christ, man! I should have my head examined, still fuckin' around with you! I mean it! You don't listen! You never listen! I swear, man, teachin' my dog was easier than tryin' to teach you!"*

Diggy was still turned away when Stick said, "I'm sorry, Dig."

Diggy turned around to face his friend, looking at him through tired eyes. "I know. I done heard that shit before. You're sorry. And hell, I believe you mean it. I think you really do feel bad for bein' such a pathetic motherfucker over her. I think you honestly can't help it. There's somethin' in your brain that won't let you just walk away, that won't accept the fact that it's over."

"I don't want her back," Stick said. "Hell, I couldn't even have her if I did. I mean, look, we're in Hades."

"You couldn't have her anyway, even if we wasn't here! That's what I'm tryin' ta tell you!"

"I just want to apologize," Stick said. "Just say I'm sorry and leave things on good terms." He paused. "As good as they can be anyway."

"You're like a broken record, man. How many times have you apologized?"

Stick stared at him, saying nothing.

"And after all that apologizin', what's changed?" Diggy said. "What has all that apologizin' got your ass? Nothin'. Not a fuckin' thing."

CHAPTER SIXTY-FOUR

Luckily, they reached the building where the Oracle was supposed to be without encountering the Vikings. When they found the building, which looked abandoned, sporting an older-than-dirt broken neon sign that said HOTEL out front, Stick said, "This is the place."

Diggy said, "Alright." He sighed, knowing full well that Stick was blowing his opportunity. "You see them steps over there, under that roof across the street? That looks like a dry spot. You go do your thing, and I'll be sittin' there, waitin' for your ass. But try to hurry some, okay?"

"I don't know if I can."

"Just try. Don't leave me out here to marinate."

They bumped fists and walked in different directions.

Stick went to the boarded-up door and knocked, just as Swearengen had told him to. When no one answered, Stick banged on the door, harder this time. Still no one came, so Stick banged harder still.

Stick looked across the street at Diggy, already sitting on the steps and out of the rain and pointed his machete at the door. As he was doing this, the door opened. He turned back around and saw a short Chinese man peering out at him. "Yes?"

Stick was confused. Could this be Horsecock? He'd always been told that Chinese men had tiny peckers.

"Are you Horsecock?"

The man nodded. "Yes. I am Horsecock."

Stick nodded, thinking the stereotype must be wrong. Before he could speak, Horsecock looked at the machete in his hand with a worried expression. "Why is this?"

"No, no," Stick assured him. "It's not for you. It's for safety."

Horsecock looked down the road in the direction they'd come from. "Yes. There are many dangerous men on the streets." Then he leaned in as if he was sharing a secret with Stick and whispered, *"Vikings."*

Stick nodded. "Vikings! Exactly."

Horsecock stared at him silently as if he was waiting for something. Then Stick remembered.

"Simon says."

Horsecock just stared at him, saying nothing.

"Simon says," Stick repeated, louder this time.

When Horsecock still didn't respond, Stick said, "Al Swearengen sent me."

The mention of Swearengen's name brought Horsecock to life and he nodded, opening the door. "Please come in." Horsecock stood by the door, and then closed it when Stick was inside.

"You are here for Oracle, yes?"

"Yes."

"Please to follow me." Horsecock opened another door and stepped down onto a stairway. He turned to look at Stick again. "Please close door behind." As Stick stepped down to follow him, he wondered how exactly the language translation worked. If everyone heard everything in their own language, then why did Horsecock and Belochkin speak in broken English? But that was a question for later. Right now, there were more important things to focus on.

CHAPTER SIXTY-FIVE

After they'd taken several flights of stairs and gone through several doors, they came to yet another. Horsecock turned and looked at Stick. "This is Oracle." Horsecock knocked a fancy knock—obviously a code. Horsecock waited for a moment, then opened the door. Inside, Stick found a room filled with technology he didn't know or recognize. There were giant machines with blinking lights and wires spread everywhere. To the left of that, there was a metallic chair that seemed to be attached to the machines.

There was a large black man standing guard in the room. He had a scar running down his face and through a milky, yellow-ish eye. He was holding a hatchet similar to the one Diggy had been carrying. He looked at Stick's machete and nodded at it. "I'll be taking that." Stick shrugged, said, "Sure thing, boss," and handed over the machete.

"You can leave him," came a man's voice from their right. Stick looked and saw a Jewish man in his thirties with a curly Jew 'fro and a full beard, wearing a white coat like the ones the orderlies had worn at the way station.

"I go now," Horsecock said, and Stick heard the door close behind him.

The Jewish man approached Stick with a big smile on his face. He stuck out his hand for Stick to shake. "Hi, I'm Ronald!" he said enthusiastically.

Stick shook his hand, narrowing his eyes. "*Ronald?...You're* the Oracle?"

The Jewish man laughed a goofy laugh and pointed toward the machines.

"Not really," he said. "*That's* the Oracle."

Stick stared at the machines, trying to understand. "So the Oracle isn't a person?"

"No," Ronald said, laughing again. "It's a machine."

Stick stared at him for a moment, considering whether or not he should ask the question he wanted to ask. Finally, he decided fuck it, he'd ask. Stick pointed his thumb back at the door behind. "The Chinese guy..."

"Horsecock?"

"Yeah. Why do they call him that?"

Ronald giggled a little. "What can I say? They say he's hung like a horse."

"*Really?*"

Ronald shrugged and held his hands out to his sides. "I can't verify it as a fact. I mean, I've never actually *seen* the guy's cock."

"But I thought—"

"I know, I know," Ronald said, grinning big. "I've heard that too, but I'm no expert on Chinese dicks."

"So if you're not the Oracle, then who are you?" Stick asked.

"I told you. I'm Ronald."

"No. I mean, what do you do here?"

Ronald's grin half-slipped away. "Look, man, I've got shit to do today, I don't have a lot of time. Do you wanna stand here yapping about my boring-ass life and Chinamen's peckers, or do you wanna take a spin in this baby and go back to Earth?"

CHAPTER SIXTY-SIX

Once Stick was sitting in the metal chair, Ronald placed a metal band around his head and spent a moment tightening it to fit snugly.

"You've got a little head, man," Ronald said.

Having never considered this before, Stick asked, "I do?"

"Compared to some guys. I had a guy in here the other day, great big guy, had a head as big as a globe." Ronald messed with the straps for another moment before saying, "I don't know if this was from your time or not, but did you ever see *Pee-wee's Playhouse?*"

Stick blinked. "The TV show?"

"*Yeah!*" Ronald said enthusiastically. "Yeah! Do you remember, there was this guy on there who had a globe for a head?"

"Globie," Stick said. "His name was Globie."

"*Right!* Well, the guy who was in here the other day...his head was so big, so round, it reminded me of Globie."

Ronald attached some electrodes to Stick's face and chest. When he was done, he stepped back and looked at Stick, admiring his handiwork.

"Okay," Ronald said. "I'm gonna explain how this all works, okay?"

Stick nodded.

"I can put you within a two-mile radius of the place on Earth you want to go—"

"Two miles?"

Ronald nodded. "I know. It's a pain in the ass, but it's what we've got, and it's better than nothing. Now, when you get there, you're gonna enter someone else's body and take it over."

"Like a possession?"

Ronald laughed his goofy laugh again. "Yeah, it's like that. Exactly like that. There's no way to say whose body it will be, just like there's no way to say exactly where you're gonna end up. It's not an exact science. But this should get you close enough to whatever or whoever you're going back to see that you can find your way there. This takes you back to current time, *right now.* Since you know about *Pee-wee's Playhouse,* I guess you're fine with that. This is gonna be your time. Some guys go back—guys who've been dead for a long-ass time—and they see things they don't understand, and they come back looking sort of shell-shocked. But you should be just fine."

"So tell me again," Stick said, "how long am I gonna have there?"

"That's not an exact science either."

"Just give me a ballpark figure."

"It's usually somewhere between an hour and three hours. That should give you enough time to do what you need to do." Ronald stared at him. "So, are you ready?"

"I'm ready," Stick said.

CHAPTER SIXTY-SEVEN

Stick closed his eyes and he heard Ronald pushing buttons. This was followed by a loud whooshing sound, which seemed to get louder and louder, the sound of something moving faster and faster. Stick kept his eyes clenched.

And suddenly…

there was no sound.

At all.

Stick opened his eyes from the darkness only to find more darkness.

What was this?

He looked around but saw nothing.

"Hello?" Stick said, hearing his new voice for the first time. It sounded strange to him. Hearing that new and different voice increased his anxiety and he spoke again, sounding frantic. *"Hellooo?!"*

He heard a woman's soft voice. "What's wrong, Mr. Conway?"

"I…I…," he struggled.

"Yes?" the woman asked with concern in her voice.

"I can't see anything."

There was a long pause. The woman said, "You're blind, Mr. Conway. You know that."

Shit! Had he really taken over the body of a blind man? *Jesus fuck!* He had the worst luck! This would complicate matters tremendously.

Now that he was aware of the situation, he could feel and recognize that he was lying in a bed beneath a blanket. He reached down and felt around to check if he had any clothes on. His hands felt boxer shorts, but nothing else.

"Are you sure I'm blind?" he asked, realizing the question was moronic before it even left his mouth. Well, Mr. Conway's mouth.

The woman spoke, sounding as if she were on the verge of laughter. "Of course I'm sure, Mr. Conway. Are you okay? You seem…"

He thought she was going to say crazy. *You seem fucking crazy.*

But she didn't.

Instead, she said, "a little bit off today."

YES, YOU BITCH!, he thought. *I'M TOTALLY FUCKING OFF! IN FACT, I'M NOT EVEN MR. CONWAY!*

"Okay," he managed. "Where am I?"

"What do you mean?"

"Our location. Where exactly are we?"

"We're at your house, Mr. Conway," the woman said. "In your bedroom."

"So…"

"What, Mr. Conway?"

"Who are you?"

"I'm Marjorie. Don't you remember?"

"Okay, Marjorie," he said, becoming more flustered by the second. "Who are you? Are we family?"

"I'm your nurse. You know that. Your wife hired me to take care of you."

"Well, where is she?"

"Who?"

"My wife."

"Uh, she passed away, Mr. Conway. Don't you remember?"

Stick was starting to get the hang of this.

"Do I have a car?" he asked.

"No. You're...*blind*."

"Right, right. My wife, did she have a car?"

"Uh, yeah, she had a Saab. It's out in the garage."

"Can you drive me somewhere, Marjorie?"

She paused. "Well, uh...I don't have a driver's license. Remember?"

No, bitch, I don't remember.

"Who else is here?" Stick asked.

"Where?"

He was becoming really flustered now. The clock was ticking.

"In the fucking house!" he yelled. *"Where do you think?!"*

"I'm...I'm sorry, Mr. Conway," she said, on the verge of tears.

"No, no," Stick said, trying to fix the situation. "It's my fault. I'm not feeling well." He paused. "But...is there anyone else here?"

"No, but I can call my boyfriend. He could come get us. He has a lunch break in a couple of hours."

A couple of hours? No, that wouldn't work.

This wasn't going the way Stick had pictured it.

Tick-tock! Tick-fucking-Tock! Time was slipping away.

He'd have to change plans.

"Marjorie."

"Yes, Mr. Conway?"

"Could you be a doll and get me the phone?"

"Uh, sure, Mr. Conway. Hold on a moment."

It took about thirty seconds and then Marjorie was back.

"I've got it, Mr. Conway. Would you like me to dial the number?"

"Yes," he said. "Dial the number and then be a dear and give me a few minutes alone."

CHAPTER SIXTY-EIGHT

Stick held the phone to his ear. It was a landline. It took a few seconds to start ringing.

It rang once. No answer.

It rang twice. No answer.

It rang a third time. No an—

"Hello?" came a man's voice. Stick knew that voice, recognized it immediately—*it was Keeling!* Who was he to answer Tina's phone? Stick considered saying something hateful but remembered his mission. He had to stay focused.

"Hello, sir," Stick said with his new voice. "Could I speak with Tina?"

There was a brief pause. "Can I tell her who's calling?"

"Conway."

"Conway?"

Not knowing Conway's first name, Stick said, *"Jerry* Conway."

"Can I tell her what it's regarding?"

"It's a sensitive matter. It's about her husband."

"She's not married anymore."

Jesus Christ on a popsicle stick! Stick obviously knew they were divorced, but hearing this sonofabitch say it made him feel sick.

"Right," Stick said. "I meant to say her *ex*-husband."

"What has he done now?"

Ugh. Stick hated him so much.

"Is she there?" Stick asked.

"Yeah, okay," Keeling said. "I'll get her."

There was a pause as Keeling carried the phone to Tina. Stick heard him quietly say, "It's for you. Some guy. Says it's about Stick." He paused before saying, "Hell if I know."

Tina got on the phone.

"Hello?" Hearing her voice melted something in his heart and Stick found himself on the verge of tears.

"Tina," he said, his voice cracking.

"Who is this?" she asked, already irritated.

Stick almost said his name but stopped himself. "Jerry Conway."

"This is about Dwayne?"

It was strange hearing her say his name. He hadn't heard her call him by that name in years, so it was slightly foreign.

"Yes, ma'am," Stick said, regaining his composure. "He wanted me to call and give you a message."

Long pause. "Why can't he call me himself?"

Good question and, weirdly enough, an obvious one Stick hadn't considered.

"He, uh...He knew you would be mad at him, so he wanted me to call."

"I'm hanging up."

"No," Stick said. "Please don't. This'll only take a minute."

He heard her blow out air. "Fine. What's the message?"

"First, he says you won't see him again," Stick said, hoping this would have an effect on her. It did, but it was the wrong effect.

"Good," she said. "Is that it?"

Stick felt ill. This wasn't what he was hoping to hear.

"Tina," he said, realizing again he couldn't speak as himself.

"Where is he?"

"He wanted me to tell you that you won't have to worry about him messing things up for you anymore."

She laughed a sarcastic, angry laugh. "That would be a first."

"The other thing he wanted me to tell you was that he's sorry for everything he's done and that he loves you more than you could ever know."

This did not achieve the desired effect either.

"Is that all?"

"Yes," Stick said, repeating, "He loves you very, very much."

"You listen and you listen good, whoever you are. If you talk to Dwayne again, you tell him that I'm glad he's going wherever he's going and that I'd be happy to never see or hear from him again. Do you hear me?"

Crystal clear.

"All he's ever done is fuck things up for me," Tina said.

"That can't be true."

"Oh, it is. It fucking is."

"But there were good times," Stick said.

"Very few. Very, very few. Let me tell you, the good times did not outweigh the bad. Not at all. Not even fucking close. So you go back and you tell Dwayne that he could die a fiery death for all I care. Tell him to just fuck off and never bother me again."

Hearing these words hurt him. Hurt him bad.

Diggy was right. Stick had known he was right, but he'd hoped he was wrong.

"Is there anything else you want me to tell him?" Stick asked.

"Tell him I hate him."

Stick paused, taking a breath.

"Tina?"

She didn't answer.

"Before I let you go, I have one last thing to say," Stick said.

"Make it quick."

"Tell Keeling he's a dirty cop and a piece of shit. Tell him if I ever see him, I'm going to beat the shit out of him again. And you—"

"Stick? Is that you?"

"You're a cunt," he said, clicking off.

CHAPTER SIXTY-NINE

Sitting in darkness, Stick felt the tears cascading down his cheeks. He wiped them away with the back of his hand.

"*Marjorie!*" he called.

A minute later, the nurse was back. "Yes, Mr. Conway?"

"I need you to dial another number for me."

He told her he didn't know the number and asked her if she would look it up on her phone. She said yes, promptly located the number, dialed it, and handed the phone back.

"I'm gonna need you to step out again," Stick said.

"Sure thing," Marjorie said. "No problem."

And like that, she was gone.

The phone started to ring, and it was answered immediately.

"Croissants & Coffee, this is Dave."

"Hello, Dave," Stick said. "Is Jimmy working today?"

"Yes, he is."

"Could I speak with him?"

"Yeah, sure, hold on a moment."

Stick sat and listened, hearing bustling noises on the other end of the line. After a moment, his son answered. "Hello, this is Jimmy."

"Jim," Stick said.

Jimmy recognized something in the voice, maybe the cadence. "*Dad?*"

"Don't hang up, Jim. I've got something I need to say."

"I'm busy, Dad, and I don't want to talk to you."

"That's fine. I'll do all the talking. Just give me a minute."

"One minute, and that's it."

"I love you very much, Jim. I know I wasn't a very good father, but—"

"You were a piece of shit."

"Listen, Jim, I only have a minute. No matter what you think, I love you very much. I know I've been...*lacking*, to say the least. If I were you, I wouldn't want to talk to me either. After this, you'll never have to again. Listen, Jim, I'm sorry I didn't say the right things when you came out."

Stick paused for a moment to feel out the situation, but Jimmy said nothing.

"I've had a lot of time to think about it," Stick said.

"And what did you figure out?" Jimmy asked with an angry tone.

"That I love you and I don't care if you're gay or straight. None of that matters. What matters is that you're my son and I love you. I will always love you, no matter what. I mean it. I would even love you if you were a Republican."

Stick waited for the laugh, but there wasn't one.

"You're a tough crowd, Jim," Stick said.

"What do you expect, Dad? That because you said you're sorry, that suddenly everything you said and the way you reacted would disappear? That I would just forgive you, and like that, we'd become besties?"

"I don't need to be your bestie. I just want you to know that I love you."

"Are you finished?"

"I guess so, Jim. I'm trying here."

Jimmy hung up. Stick thought he'd heard him hang up but wasn't sure.

"Jim? Are you there, Jim?"

CHAPTER SEVENTY

Stick sighed and set the phone on his chest. He called for Marjorie. When she came, he asked, "What kind of food is in the fridge?"

"What do you mean?"

"Just tell me. What do we have in there? Do we have any ice cream?"

"Yes, I believe so. Do you want me to bring you some?"

"Please," Stick said. "Bring me the whole carton and a spoon." He paused before adding, "Marjorie?"

"Yes?"

"Bring me the ice cream and whatever other sweets are in the cupboard."

"Are you sure?"

"Oh yeah, I'm definitely sure. I feel like I haven't had sweets in a while, and I'm starving."

"Okay, Mr. Conway."

"Is there any soda?"

"Soda?" she asked. "You mean pop?"

"Yeah, pop."

"I think there's some root beer."

"Okay, bring me that too."

If he couldn't accomplish anything else while he was here, he figured he could at least enjoy food. He'd missed it, especially ice cream and sweets.

CHAPTER SEVENTY-ONE

They were making the long trek back to the Gem when Diggy said, "Wouldn't it have been nice if somebody coulda told you ahead 'a time that Tina was gonna be a bitch? That she didn't love you no more?" He put his hand to his chin, pretending to ponder this. "Yeah, that woulda been nice. *But wait!* Now that I think about it, somebody did tell you that exact thing."

Still walking, Stick nodded. "What can I say? You did."

"What can you say? You can say I told you so."

"I just said that."

"You said it but not in those words. I wanna hear it in them exact words."

"Whatever."

Diggy chuckled.

"Yeah, well, you also told me to call Jim," Stick said. "And that didn't go well either."

"Yeah, but that coulda gone either way," Diggy said. "There was no question about how the talk with Tina was gonna go."

Stick shrugged. "I don't know."

Diggy looked at him. "You can't blame the kid, though."

"Way to support your brother!"

"Well, it's true," Diggy said. "I told you if you treated him like shit when he came out, you were gonna end up payin' for that shit in the long run."

"You did say that."

"You're right, I did," Diggy said. "But you know what else I told you?"

When Stick didn't respond, Diggy repeated his question more adamantly. "I said, do you know what else I told your ass?!"

Stick rolled his eyes. "You tell me so much shit it's hard to remember it all."

"Well then," Diggy said, "let me remind you. I told you way back when that boy was, what? Twelve? Thirteen? I told you he was gay. *I told you*, but you were all 'nah, Dig, not my boy. Not Jim.'"

"How was I supposed to know?"

Diggy turned and glared at him. "Motherfucker, I knew. And you knew the boy better than I did, so you shoulda known. Fuckin' Ray Charles coulda seen it. And he's blind and dead."

"So what?"

"So you coulda listened back then and prepared yourself. You coulda got your mind right before he came out. Maybe then you wouldn't 'a fucked it all up."

"Woulda, coulda, motherfucking shoulda. It's too late to do anything about it now."

Diggy turned to Stick. "You shoulda listened, Stick. You shoulda—"

"Be quiet," Stick said, staring off in the distance.

"What the fuck?"

Stick raised the machete and used it to point at a group of men standing on the curb half a block ahead. "Look, Dig."

Diggy squinted his eyes, trying to see through the rain. "You think that's them Viking fucks?"

"I don't know. It's too dark to see for sure."

Diggy raised the hatchet to his chest and tapped its blade against the palm of his other hand.

"I hope it's them," Diggy said. "I got somethin' for their asses."

They kept walking, getting closer and closer to the men. They still couldn't make out the men's faces, but they could see their movements change when they noticed Diggy and Stick approaching. They could see their bodies tensing up.

Diggy said, "Yeah, that's them."

"I see the helmets now."

"And I see the fucker that punched me in the balls," Diggy said.

"I think they all punched us in the balls," Stick said.

"He was the first."

"The first always counts twice."

One of the Vikings spoke. "You come back for more?"

There was a titter of laughter among his comrades.

"Yessir," Diggy said, gripping the hatchet tightly. "We're back for more."

"I shouldn't hang out with you anymore," Stick said. "You always get me into trouble."

CHAPTER SEVENTY-TWO

They were walking again, their clothes covered in dark blood.

Looking down at his once-white jacket, Diggy said, "I'm gonna have to get a new outfit. This shit is fucked up."

Stick nodded. "Mine looks bad too."

"Yeah," Diggy said, "but to be fair, your clothes looked like shit already."

Stick nodded in agreement.

"At least I got my fuckin' shoes back," Diggy said. "Even if they got blood all over 'em."

"One of those fuckers cut my arm. Sliced it like a butcher cutting meat."

"Well, you got him back pretty good."

Stick nodded, grinning. "He won't be cutting any arms now."

"I suspect not," Diggy said, starting to chuckle. "Man, oh man, you didn't have to cut his head off."

"And you didn't have to hurl it down the street."

"We shoulda kept it for a souvenir."

"Yeah, but where would we put it?" Stick said. "I don't know that I have any place to display a head in my apartment that would look quite right."

"Did you see the other dude's head split open when I hit him with the hatchet?"

"It was kind of hard to miss."

"I got him good, though, didn't I?"

"You did," Stick said. "You got him good."

"Hell, we got all of 'em good."

CHAPTER SEVENTY-THREE

Diggy was standing near the edge of a cliff, and, to his surprise, the sun was out and it was as bright as he could remember having ever seen it. It was also hot, but he welcomed the heat as it came with the sunlight. Then he realized his twenty-one-year-old daughter, Alyssa, was standing at the edge of a cliff about twenty feet away on his right.

She turned and looked at him. There were tears in her eyes.

"Help me, Daddy!"

Diggy knew something was wrong immediately. There was a sinking feeling in his stomach, and he knew to look to his left. When he looked, he saw his seventy-something-aged daddy, also standing close to the cliff's edge.

Daddy seemed to know Diggy was staring at him, as if he could feel his gaze. He turned toward Diggy with a sad look in his eyes.

Diggy didn't know how he knew, but he did, that they were both in danger. He also knew Benny Cordella was behind it. He knew without being told that he could save only one of them.

Had he been faced with this choice in his waking life, Diggy would have been forced to choose Alyssa. He loved his daddy, but his daddy had lived a full life—fuller than most—and Alyssa was still a baby. *His* baby. But here, in the dream, he couldn't see the logic, and the choice was difficult, so he stood there, looking back and forth at them.

"I love you, Bobby," Daddy said. Diggy saw that there were tears in his eyes too.

"Daddy," he said. "I don't know what to do. I don't know—"

He was suddenly awakened by someone knocking on the door to his apartment. Tired and feeling discombobulated since he'd been ripped from the dream, which had seemed very real, he made his way to the door.

This better not be some bullshit.

Just before he reached the door, the person knocked again.

"Alright, alright," Diggy muttered.

He unlocked the door and pulled it open, finding Stick and Swearengen standing in the hall.

Diggy rubbed his eyes. "What the hell, man? I'm tryin' ta get some sleep here."

"Al's got something for us," Stick said.

Diggy looked at Swearengen. "Whatchu got?"

Swearengen smiled big. "I got what you asked for."

Still half asleep, Diggy rubbed his head. "Huh?"

"Dread Corbin," Stick said.

Diggy looked at Swearengen again. "You found him?"

"Yes, sir," Swearengen said. "I found him."

CHAPTER SEVENTY-FOUR

The address Swearengen gave them was forty-some blocks away, but in the opposite direction of their two previous trips. Swearengen told them to ask for Martin Donaldson. Donaldson was a second-tier crime boss, and Dread Corbin was one of his men. "I worked out a deal," Swearengen said. "I made a deal with Donaldson. When you get there, he'll give you Corbin." When they asked him what kind of deal he'd worked out, Swearengen just winked and said, "Don't you worry your pretty little heads. All you need to know is that it has to do with a shitload of kamur."

Diggy and Stick were walking again, armed with the same hatchet and machete they had used to slaughter the Vikings.

"I'm tired of all this walkin'," Diggy said. "Why's everything spaced out so damned far?"

"And why aren't there cars here?" Stick complained again.

"A-fuckin'-men! We need a car."

"Or Uber. Wouldn't it be nice to be able to just call someone and have them come pick us up?"

They walked another two blocks without speaking. Stick broke the silence. "Have you decided who you're going to see when you get your turn with the Oracle?"

Diggy looked off in the distance, thinking. "I'll probably see Alyssa. I love my daddy, but I think I should see my baby girl."

"Probably so."

"You know," Diggy said, "I had a dream last night. I was still havin' it when you and Swearengen showed up at my door, knockin' like you the damn cops."

"We are cops," Stick said.

"You *wish* we were still cops. Anyhow, Alyssa and Daddy was there."

"In the dream?"

Diggy gave him a pissy look. "No, in my apartment. Whatchu think, man?"

Stick nodded. It was a stupid question.

"They was both there, and one of 'em was gon' fall off a cliff," Diggy said. "And I was the only one could stop 'em from fallin', but I could only save one of 'em. The other one had to go."

"Off the cliff," Stick said.

"Exactly.

"Why were they there?"

Diggy looked at him. "In the dream?"

"On the cliff?"

"How the fuck should I know?"

"It's your fucking dream!"

"Yeah, but listen. Benny was there."

"Benny?" Stick asked.

"Yeah, but I couldn't see him."

"But you heard his voice?"

"Nah," Diggy said. "He didn't speak."

"Then how did you know he was there?"

"Man," Diggy said, "would you just shut up and listen? I don't know how I knew Benny was the one makin' 'em jump, but I did. You know how dreams are. They don't make sense."

"One time I had a dream that I was naked in the middle of the station house with my dick hanging out," Stick said.

"You really did that," Diggy said. "That was real."

Stick thought about it. "I don't remember that."

"Yeah, you do. You just think it was a dream because you

202

was drunk as a wino with a tax return."

"When was this?"

"Listen, man," Diggy said, turning toward him with big, angry eyes. "I was talkin' about *my* dream, alright?"

"Alright, alright."

"So I was thinkin'. I'm pretty sure the dream was about my havin' to choose who I'm goin' to see when I go back."

"Where does Benny figure into that?"

"I'm not sure. Maybe it's cause he's the one who sent us here, which is why I'm in the position of havin' to choose."

"You're a regular Sigmund Freud," Stick said.

"I prefer to think of myself more as Dr. Phil," Diggy said.

"Dr. Phil? That guy sucks."

"I'm like a badass Dr. Phil," Diggy said. "I'm a dude that'll get psychological on your ass and then beat the shit outta you after I'm done."

"I've never seen Dr. Phil beat the shit out of anyone."

They walked a few blocks without speaking again. Finally, Stick said, "So, tell me about when I was naked at the station house. You sure that's true?"

"It was during the Christmas party a few years back."

Stick squinted his eyes, trying to make himself remember.

"It was the night you fucked Connie Kuchinski," Diggy said.

Stick stopped and looked at him with a shocked expression. "Wait," he said. "I fucked Connie Kuchinski?"

"You did, you nasty motherfucker, you did."

"How do you know? Maybe I didn't actually do it."

"You did it."

"How do you know?"

Diggy looked at him. "'Cause you fucked her big ass on top 'a one of them desks in the bullpen."

"Hmmm," Stick said. "I hope it was Keeling's desk."

CHAPTER SEVENTY-FIVE

They were still walking through the rain and darkness when they saw it.

Right before that, they were still talking shit. Because that's what Diggy and Stick did best.

"You know," Diggy said, "I been thinkin'."

"That's good to hear."

"No, seriously, Stick. You've seen *The Exorcist*, right?"

"The movie?"

"Of course, the movie," Diggy said. "What else would it be?"

"I've seen it about fifty times. What about it?"

"Remember how that demon got inside that little girl's body and possessed her?"

"Kinda," Stick said sarcastically. "I mean, that is a pretty significant plot point."

"When you went back to Earth, you was kinda like that demon, except you was takin' over a blind dude's body instead of little girl's."

Stick nodded. "What if possessions are really just people going back with the Oracle?"

"That would be interesting, but that wouldn't work."

"Why's that?"

"Because that demon stayed in that little bitch's body for a long time," Diggy said. "Weeks, I think."

"I think it was a couple of months."

"See, that wouldn't work because the Oracle only lets you go back for an hour or two."

Stick considered this. "Maybe that's the way it really happens, but when they make those movies, they exaggerate the length of time. You know, to make it more exciting."

"Maybe. But the way I see it, you fucked up."

"What did I do this time?"

"You coulda made your head spin and puked out some pea soup like that little girl," Diggy said. "But not you. What did your ass do? You went and ate some fuckin' ice cream!"

"It was damn good ice cream, too. Neapolitan."

"Neapolitan?" Diggy asked.

"What's wrong with Neapolitan?"

"It's nasty. Who the fuck wants strawberry ice cream mixed in with the chocolate and the vanilla? That shit is gross, man. G-R-O-S-S, gross."

They walked for another three blocks in silence, and then Stick spoke. "It's boring walking around all the time. We need something to pass the time."

"We talkin'. Ain't that enough?"

"I mean like a game," Stick said. "Something like slug bug. You remember slug bug?"

"That game where you punch somebody every time you see one of them ugly little cars?"

"Yeah, that one. You hit them and say 'slug bug' whenever you see a Volkswagon."

"That's some dumb shit, Stick. I'm pretty sure that's a white people game, like that be quiet game. Both of those games suck hairy donkey balls. Besides, ain't no cars here for us to look out for."

"Then we'd have to punch each other every time we saw something else."

Diggy looked at him. "Like what? What do they have a lot of here that we would see fairly consistently?"

Stick considered this. "Assholes," he said. "There's no

shortage of those."

"I'd have to hit you every two seconds, so that ain't gon' work."

"Why would you have to do that?"

"Because I see you every place I go," Diggy said, "and you the biggest asshole there is."

Stick was about to respond when it happened.

Diggy stopped. "Look up ahead, Stick. Do you see what I fuckin' see?"

Seeing it too, Stick said, "Jesus, Dig."

CHAPTER SEVENTY-SIX

There was movement in the street ahead, and there were a number of animals moving around in the darkness. That alone was enough to frighten them, but when a few of the creatures wandered past a streetlight, Diggy and Stick saw that it was a pack of wild ballywonks.

"How many you figure there are? Diggy asked.

"Six, maybe seven, as far as I can tell."

"You think we should we run?"

"No," Stick said. "Those fuckers run fast and they're likely to be set off by the sight of us running."

"Then what?"

"We fight them."

"*Fight them?*" Diggy said. "Are you crazy?"

"We've got weapons, Dig. A machete and a hatchet could do wonders to a ballywonk."

"Problem is, there's a bunch of 'em."

"Maybe they won't bother us if we just stand still."

"Let's hope," Diggy said. And that was the moment—almost as if they were triggered by the words—the ballywonks began charging toward them.

"Oh fuck," Stick said. That was all he could say, and there was no time to add anything more meaningful. Within seconds, the first ballywonk was launching toward him. Out of instinct more than thought, Stick moved to his left and swung the machete. He managed to avoid impact with the creature on the left side of his body, but the ballywonk collided with his right shoulder, biting into it. Stick let out a yelp as he fell back onto the pavement with the creature on top of him. Luckily, he managed to keep hold of the machete.

The creature's big teeth came at his face quickly, but Stick shielded his head with his left arm. His shoulder was hurting, his back was hurting, and the weight of the ballywonk had knocked the wind out of him. Nevertheless, he brought the machete up from the creature's left—his right—and sliced hard into its back. The pain caught the ballywonk off guard, and it stepped back a moment to evaluate what had happened. When it did, it caught the blade of the machete swooping down into its face. The creature yelped and backed off.

Stick tried to stand, but another ballywonk came at him from the right. The creature was running, close to him now, when Stick swung the bloody blade of the machete up into its neck. Now the second ballywonk yelped and fell back, allowing Stick to get on his feet.

To his right, Diggy was fighting off a couple of ballywonks himself. He had struck one of them in the side of the head with the hatchet but had then found himself unable to pull the blade out of the creature's head. As he was attempting to free the blade, the second ballywonk came at him. Diggy had timed his kick just right, despite his swinging the dying ballywonk attached to his hatchet, and he kicked the second ballywonk in his chest hard enough to knock him back. The first ballywonk was still whimpering when Diggy managed to pull the hatchet blade free from its head. Diggy knew the ballywonk's death was a foregone conclusion, so he let it fall to the ground.

He turned his attention to the ballywonk he'd kicked, which was now coming again, baring its sharp teeth and growling. Diggy tried to position his feet properly in preparation for the attack, but he tripped over the thrashing tail of the dying bally-wonk on the ground. Similar to Stick's encounter, Diggy fell back onto the pavement with the ballywonk colliding with him on his way down.

Diggy immediately felt a searing pain making its way down his face, from his forehead to his lower cheek, just missing his eye. The pain was sharp and Diggy knew at once the creature had sliced his face with its claws.

"Motherfucker!" Diggy growled, kneeing the thing hard. That made the creature pause for the briefest of seconds, but then its yellow eyes became visibly angrier. He swung the hatchet blade upward as hard as he could, but in that moment, a running ballywonk came out of nowhere, colliding with the creature and knocking it off Diggy's chest. In an instant, the two crazed ballywonks were locked in an all-out fight a foot away.

Diggy leaped to his feet and slammed the blade of the hatchet down into the back of one of their heads, and the damned thing let out a sound like a scream and dropped to the ground, the blade coming loose from its back. The ballywonk started to turn, and Diggy jumped on it before it could, bringing the hatchet blade down hard into its face. This one didn't growl, howl, or moan. It just died.

There was no time for Diggy to celebrate his victory as another ballywonk rushed him from the right, knocking him down again. On the pavement, Diggy didn't see Stick chop the remaining ballywonk's neck three times in quick succession.

This is how it went for the next seven or eight minutes, with the two friends fighting and killing the ballywonks one by one.

When all the creatures were slain, Diggy and Stick were lying on their backs, staring up into the rain.

"That all of 'em?" Stick asked wearily.

"It damn well better be."

"Jesus, that was something."

"One of them fuckers sliced up my face, Stick."

Stick pushed a dead ballywonk off his legs and pushed himself up off the ground. "How bad is it?" he asked.

Diggy was still on the ground, touching his wound. "It ain't good."

"Don't forget, wounds heal themselves here."

Diggy had forgotten this. "Oh, yeah! I forgot!"

Stick reached down and gave Diggy a hand, helping him up.

As the two hobbled friends made their way down the street, Diggy said, "Fucker done tore up my pretty face."

"I hate to break this to you, Dig, but you weren't pretty to begin with."

CHAPTER SEVENTY-SEVEN

Their wounds had not yet healed when they reached the building where Martin Donaldson's crew was supposed to be. The place looked nondescript—no signs, no one standing guard outside. It looked like a regular old, run-of-the-mill apartment building.

Diggy looked at Stick. "You sure this is it?"

"This is the address."

They stood in the rain for a moment, Diggy looking down the street one way, Stick the other. Finally, Stick said, "Alright, let's do this."

As they approached the building's stoop, Stick said, "It's not too late to turn back, Dig. We could just leave Dread Corbin alone and no one would ever be the wiser. Even better, we'd be safe."

"You don't think we safe?"

"I never feel safe when I'm with you," Stick said. "But let me guess, you still want to do this."

"You know I do. You *know* I do. I gave my fuckin' word, Stick. Ain't no goin' back on it now."

Standing in front of the wooden door, Stick shook his head and knocked.

The door opened almost immediately. There was a big, tough-looking sonofabitch who looked African standing there.

"Yeah?" the big fucker asked.

"We're here to see Mr. Donaldson," Stick said.

The man tilted his head and squinted his eyes like he was trying to look through Stick. "What for?"

"Business," Diggy said.

"What kinda business?"

"The mind-your-own-fuckin-business kinda business," Diggy said.

The big fucker's eyebrows lowered until they were as straight as a heterosexual caterpillar, and there was pure, unadulterated anger in his eyes. He stepped outside with his chest puffed out. "You don't want none of this."

Diggy stepped forward. Recognizing the impending pissing match, Stick put his hand up and stepped between them, staring into the big fucker's eyes. "Al Swearengen sent us."

The big fucker raised an eyebrow and tilted his head back. Then he nodded and stepped aside. "Why didn't you just say so to begin with? The boss is expecting you. He thought you were gonna be here a bit ago."

Diggy pointed at the bloody claw marks on his face. "We got sidetracked."

"Vikings?"

"Ballywonks."

"I don't fuck with ballywonks."

"We wasn't tryin' 'a fuck with them either," Diggy said. "But the ballywonks had other ideas."

"Why don't you fellas come in," the big fucker said, ushering them in.

When Diggy and Stick stepped inside, they found themselves looking down a long corridor with a few doors on each side and another at the far end. The big fucker closed the door behind them.

Stick asked, "This is where Donaldson's crew operates?"

"Ain't no crew," the big fucker said. "It's a criminal organization."

Stick looked at him. "Oh, well, pardon me."

"This criminal organization, it got a name?" Diggy asked.

"Yeah," the big fucker said. "They call us the East 100s."

"What the hell kinda name is that?"

The big fucker looked offended. "What do you mean?"

Stick put his hand on Diggy's shoulder, hoping to calm him.

"It's a shit name," Diggy said. "Horrible. Just horrible."

The big fucker just stood there staring at him. "What do you think would be a better name?"

"*Anything*," Diggy said, chuckling. "Literally *anything*. You could call yourselves the Fuckin' Weirdos and it would be a damn sight better than the East 100s. That shit sounds like a damn cigarette!"

"Let's go see the boss," the big fucker said, not the slightest bit amused. "Down at the end of the hall."

Diggy and Stick made their way down the hall toward the door at the end. The big fucker walked behind them. When they reached the door, the big fucker said, "Go ahead and knock. The boss is expecting you."

CHAPTER SEVENTY-EIGHT

Stick knocked.

"Come in," said a voice on the other side of the door.

Stick opened the door to see a large room with a man—clearly Donaldson—standing there, flanked by katana-wielding goons. As soon as Diggy laid eyes on Donaldson, he knew they were fucked.

Because of this, he said, "We're fucked."

Stick turned toward him and whispered, "What do you mean?"

"It's been a while since our paths crossed," the man said, staring at Diggy.

Stick didn't understand. He looked over at his friend. "You know this guy?"

Diggy looked at him sheepishly. "We've met before."

Stick looked back and forth between Diggy and Donaldson.

Donaldson met Stick's gaze and smiled. "What? He hasn't told you?"

Stick looked at Diggy. "What's he talking about?"

Diggy shrugged. "He's the punk fucker I beat up and stole his clothes."

"What the fuck did you do that for?"

"Good question," Donaldson said. "Why *did* you do that?"

"I needed clothes," Diggy said. "And you was actin' like an asshole."

Donaldson eyeballed Diggy's torn and dirtied clothing. "You haven't taken very good care of my clothes, I see."

Stick shook his head. "You're always getting me in trouble."

"How the hell was I supposed to know he was a crime boss?" Diggy asked. "He just looked like a regular old punk motherfucker to me."

Donaldson grinned. "Do you still think I'm a punk motherfucker?"

Diggy cracked a grin. "You really want me to answer that?"

Donaldson's smile widened. "Knock yourself out."

"Yeah," Diggy said, "you still a punk motherfucker. Hiding behind these dudes don't make you tough."

Stick raised the palm of his hand to stop him. "Dig..."

"It's makes you a punk-ass bitch," Diggy said.

CHAPTER SEVENTY-NINE

After Donaldson confirmed what they had already guessed—Swearengen had sold them out—he ordered his men to escort Diggy and Stick to a room upstairs without windows. The room was empty, except for an overhead light.

"What happens now?" Stick had asked one of the guards.

The guard had snickered and said, "Mr. Donaldson wants you locked in here until he can decide what he wants to do with you. He had planned to dip you both into a vat of acid, but your partner's smart mouth made him decide it wasn't enough."

"Two things," Diggy said. "First, y'all got a vat of acid? That's fuckin' weird. Two, he wants to do somethin' worse than dippin' our asses in a vat of acid? What the hell could be worse?"

The caused the guards to snicker.

"Trust me, he can and will come up with something worse," one of them said. "He'll come up with something so fucked up, you'll wish you'd been dipped in the acid."

"I don't deserve punishment," Stick said. "I didn't do anything. It was Dig who took his clothes."

"Mr. Donaldson don't care," the guard said. "He says you're guilty by association."

After the guards had locked them in and left, Diggy and Stick sat on the floor against the wall and contemplated their situation.

"You always get me into trouble," Stick said.

"You've gotten me in trouble lots of times," Diggy said.

"Lately it's all been you, though."

Diggy gave him a look. "*Really? You think so?* Stick, lemme ask you somethin'. Who was the dumbass who decided to get into that bar fight with Keeling? That's the shit that got us into this."

Stick returned his sour look. "Let me remind *you* of something, my oldest and dearest friend. Whose bright idea was it to steal all those AR-15s? *That* was what got us here, not the bar fight."

Knowing Stick had him, Diggy twisted his face into an angry scowl and looked at his hands, mumbling. Then, a minute or so later, he said, "I'm sorry about that. How the hell was I supposed ta know them guns belonged to Benny? As far as I knew, them dudes was just your regular old garden variety white supremacist inbred sister-fuckin' assholes."

Stick looked down for a long while, considering this. Diggy remained silent. Stick couldn't fault Dig for coming up with the plan. It wasn't like he knew the connection between the redneck fuck-ups and Benny.

Stick turned to his friend. "Hey, Dig."

"What?" Diggy said, looking down at his hands.

"I don't blame you for any of that. We got greedy. Maybe if we weren't so greedy, we wouldn't have gotten ourselves in this mess."

"I think it's like that with a lotta things, Stick. We wouldn't 'a gone through half the shit we have if it wasn't for us bein' greedy and always tryin' ta get a bigger slice of the pie."

"But that's the American Dream, Dig."

Diggy half turned his head toward him. "Ain't none of the shit we been through lately been anything like no American Dream." Then, after a moment of reconsidering, he said, "Well, I guess it is pretty American, at least from a black man's perspective."

"What do you mean?"

Diggy looked at him. "If your skin is black, America has

always been about fuckin' us over. So, with that in mind, I'd say this shit is about as American as you can get."

"As American as apple pie," Stick said.

"Fuck apple pie," Diggy said. "I prefer cherry."

"And I like chocolate cream," Stick said, "but the saying goes—"

"And sweet potato pie," Diggy continued like Stick wasn't even speaking.

"What the fuck are you talking about?"

"I'm talkin' bout pie," Diggy said indignantly. "What the fuck you think I'm talkin' about?"

"You wear me out, Dig."

Diggy grinned. "That's what ya mama say."

"Oh, brother, here we go again."

Stick was about to return the favor and throw a mom joke back when the door opened.

CHAPTER EIGHTY

It was the same two fuckers who'd brought them to the room. One of them hung back in the hallway, clutching his katana. The other man, the one with his katana sheathed, took a step toward them. He waved for them to stand, and they did.

"What the hell is this?" Diggy asked.

"Mr. Donaldson wants me to check you guys a little closer for weapons," the man said.

Stick grinned. "You sure this isn't just an excuse for you to touch our dicks?"

The man ignored this but turned his head when he heard a commotion down the hall.

"What's going on?" they heard the man in the hall ask someone.

"*We're under attack!*" someone else said.

"*Really?!*"

"*The Brotherhood of Knives is re-killing everyone they see!*" the other man shouted. "*Come on!*"

The guy in the doorway—the one with the unsheathed katana—took off running without saying a word.

This caused the guy who was about to frisk them to turn around to see what was happening. When he did, Stick rushed him, slamming him back against the wall. As the guard collided with cement, he reached for his katana, but Stick grabbed his face and slammed his head back, hard, and his head bounced off the wall. The guy started to drop, but Stick caught him. Holding him up, he reached down and slid his katana out of its scabbard. Then he let the guard drop.

Diggy went to the door to see what was happening.

"Come on," Diggy said. "The coast is clear."

They left the room and made their way down the hall. Stick led the way since he was holding the katana. A moment later, they reached a door at the end of the hall. Neither of them knew what they were looking for or where they were going.

Stick opened the door, raising his katana to strike if necessary.

There was a man inside, sitting at a desk, writing. At first they could see only his profile, but then he turned and they got a good look at him. When they did, they recognized his horribly burned face.

"You're Dread Corbin," Stick said.

Corbin looked at them with a strange expression. "And who the fuck might you be?"

"Santa Claus, bitch," Diggy said. "We came to bring you a present."

Corbin just stared at them, not understanding. He started to stand, but Stick pointed the tip of the katana at his face.

"I'd sit down if I was you," Stick said.

Corbin sat.

Diggy shut the door behind, and then turned to face Corbin.

"Benny Cordella sent us," Diggy said. "You remember him?"

Corbin's eyes got big. "Benny sent you? But *how*?"

"What do you mean?" Stick asked.

"How did Benny send you?" Corbin asked. "He sent you all the way to Hades to find me? That's insane. I don't even know how that's possible."

Diggy reached for Stick's katana. When his hands touched its handle, they shared a look. Stick let him take the sword.

"I'm about to do this motherfucker right now," Diggy said.

Corbin stared at them, his confused look now turning into an expression that said he accepted his fate.

"After what he did to Emelia, I should have known he wouldn't stop until he found me," Corbin said.

"Wait," Diggy said. "What did Benny do to Emelia?"

Corbin looked at him with sad eyes. "Emelia was my wife."

"Hold up," Stick said. "I thought Emelia was Benny's daughter."

"She was," Corbin said. "That's why we're here now."

"What do you mean?" Diggy asked.

Corbin looked at him blankly. "You don't know why you're here?"

"Why don't you just go ahead and tell us," Stick said.

"Benny and I were enemies," Corbin said. "No big thing. The job brings you almost as many enemies as it does dollars. I sent a guy to kill Benny, but he failed. That's why Emelia came to see me."

"Emelia came to see you?" Stick asked.

"Benny didn't know she was there," Corbin said. "She came to me hoping to convince me to call off the hit on her father. But then, when she came, something happened."

"Y'all fucked," Diggy said.

Corbin looked at him with a look of sincerity. "No, it wasn't like that. We talked and I was surprised how much I liked her. How much I enjoyed her company. She was smart, funny, and gorgeous." He looked at Stick. "But you guys know. You've seen her."

"Nah," Diggy said. "We've never seen her."

"Oh man, she was something," Corbin said. "She was enough to make a man believe in God." He shrugged. "Of course, I believe in God now, but back then..."

Diggy gave Stick a look, but Stick ignored him.

"We fell in love quickly," Corbin said.

"Even with your fucked up face," Diggy said.

Corbin looked at him and smiled. "Trust me, I was as shocked as you are. But it's true. She was beauty and I was her beast. She was afraid to tell Benny, and honestly, being with her was enough to make me want out of the life. So we moved down to Mexico, where we thought we could hide and live a quiet life."

"You moved to Mexico," Stick repeated, working it all out.

"We were there a couple of months, and it seemed like we were in the clear," Corbin said. "But then Benny and his guys showed up. I was out, picking up supplies a few miles away."

"Then what?" Diggy asked.

Corbin looked at him with a sad expression. If his tear ducts hadn't melted, he would have been crying. "They killed her. Very violently. And..." He stared at them for a long moment. "She was pregnant with our baby. And they—*he*—cut the baby out of her womb."

"How do you know it was Benny?" Stick asked.

"Because the sick fuck sent me a video so I could be sure it was him."

"I don't understand," Stick said. "Why did they let you live?"

"The federales showed up before they could finish. I was coming home when I saw them all out front. Because of my record and the things I'm involved in, I assumed they were there for me. So I just kept driving, thinking I would catch up with her a day or so down the line. But then, the news came out that she was dead. That our baby was..." His voice cracked. "I took off and hid out in Florida for a while. But then, one day, one of Benny's guys showed up at my place. He took me at gunpoint and made me watch a video of Benny and his pals slicing her up."

"Damn," Diggy said. "That's fucked up."

"While the guy was getting off watching the video, I over-powered him and took his gun," Corbin said. "Then I emptied the clip into his face. Needless to say, I was heartbroken. There was no reason for me to go on. Once you've known love like that—real, powerful love—it changes you forever. It changes everything about you. The way you see the world, the way you see yourself." He paused. "Plus, I knew I'd never outrun Benny.

Wherever I went and whatever I did, he was gonna be right behind me..."

"So you killed yourself," Stick said.

CHAPTER EIGHTY-ONE

They decided to take Corbin with them. The three of them walked briskly down the hall, Corbin leading the way. Stick was behind him with the katana raised to strike.

When they came to the next door, Diggy asked, "Is there a window in there?"

"Two," Corbin said.

"Good. Go ahead and open the door then."

Corbin opened it, and they stepped inside. It was another office, but there was no one there. Stick went to the window and looked down, not seeing anything but darkness and rain.

"What are we doing here?" Corbin asked.

"We about to jump," Diggy said.

"We'll break our legs if we jump."

Stick poked Corbin's throat with the blade. "Better to break your legs than lose your head."

Corbin rolled his eyes.

"Who gon' go first?" Diggy asked.

"It's gotta be you, Dig," Stick said.

Diggy looked at him like he was nuts. "And why's that?"

"He can't jump first because he's our captive," Stick said. "And I have to follow him since I've got the sword. Somebody's got to be behind him to make sure he jumps."

Diggy held his palm out. "Give me the sword then."

Stick shrugged. It didn't matter since they were all going to jump eventually.

Stick raised the glass window, which was exactly like windows back home. When the window was up, the wind blew the rain in. Stick didn't even think about it, though. By now, he was becoming as used to the rain and darkness as he was Diggy's bad attitude and his own poor decision-making. Stick climbed into the window, hanging his right leg out and letting it dangle.

"You jump after him," Stick said.

Diggy said, "No shit."

"But drop the sword before you jump," Stick said. "We don't need you getting impaled."

"Good thinking," Diggy said.

"Here goes nothing," Stick said. And he jumped. But when he fell, he unexpectedly dropped onto an awning, and he bounced. Realizing what had happened, Stick burst into laughter.

"What you laughin' about?" Diggy yelled down.

"There's an awning to break our fall!"

Stick started moving so he would be out of the way when Corbin jumped. No sooner than Stick had rolled out of the way, Corbin dropped into the same spot Stick had, and like Stick, he bounced.

The two of them scooted quickly to the edge of the awning. A moment later, they heard the katana fall onto the awning and bounce. Thirty seconds later, Diggy followed.

CHAPTER EIGHTY-TWO

They had started around the building but had seen a man come flying through a glass window. So they went back the other way. Unsure where they were going, Diggy, Stick, and Corbin walked the streets with no planned destination.

Corbin walked between them, and he kept complaining about the rain.

"It don't bother me none," Diggy said. "I got used to it pretty quick."

Stick looked at Corbin. "Why haven't you gotten used to it yet? You were here before us."

"I avoid going out," Corbin said. "So, what's the plan? Are you going to re-kill me or what?"

They walked a little farther in silence, Diggy and Stick mulling this over. Finally, Stick said, "I don't see how we can re-kill him. I think he's on the level."

Diggy said, "I hate to admit it, but I think so too."

Stick turned toward Corbin. "Benny really killed his own daughter?"

"And granddaughter."

"You already knew it was gonna be a girl?" Diggy asked.

"No, but Emelia believed it was. She even named her. She was going to be Mariella, after her great-grandmother."

There was a silence that lasted another block. Finally, Diggy said, "This changes things."

"So you're going to let me live?" Corbin said.

"Yes," Stick said. "There's no reason to re-kill you."

"What about Benny? Do you think he'll send more guys after me?"

"He'll probably be here himself before too long," Stick said.

Diggy stopped, putting his hand up. Stick and Corbin stared at him.

"I've got it," Diggy said. "I know how to make this right."

Stick asked, "How's that?"

"You know how I was tryin' ta figure out who to go see with the Oracle?" Diggy asked. "I've decided it ain't gonna be Alyssa or Daddy." He looked at Stick through the pouring rain. "I'm going after Benny."

Throwing his hands up, Stick said, "*Christ!* I wasted my trip, didn't I? I should have killed that fat fuck and made him pay for what he did."

"But how would you have killed him when you was blind?" Diggy asked.

"You're right. I guess I couldn't have."

Corbin watched this exchange.

"None of it matters now," Stick said.

"Nah, I can still go back," Diggy said. "I can handle it."

"That's what I'm saying doesn't matter."

"How you figure?"

"Swearengen turned on us," Stick said. "He was our connection to the Oracle. Without him, we don't have a way in."

"Well, shit," Diggy said, understanding now. "Maybe we can just go in there and bum rush the guy and make him do what we want him to do. We'll make him send me back, and I'll kill Benny."

Stick was skeptical. "We're going to bum rush the Oracle with what? Knives? Swords? A fucking hatchet?"

Diggy shot him an angry look. Before he could say anything, Corbin said, "I can get you in to see the Oracle."

Diggy and Stick both looked at Corbin and simultaneously

said, *"What?!"*

"I know the guy who runs the machine."

"Ronald?" Stick asked.

"Yeah, Ronald," Corbin said. "I know how you can make him do what you want."

CHAPTER EIGHTY-THREE

Corbin told them he would assist them in exchange for a favor to be asked and answered later. He had no idea when he might ask for that favor, but he assured them that when he did, it would be a big one. They agreed. "Just make sure you stay alive so you can repay me," Corbin said.

Corbin had then led them to a high-rise apartment building with a fancy neon sign announcing it as the Sherwood. He told them they would find a man named Shifty McGann there. This man, Corbin told them, was their ticket to the Oracle.

"How's that?" Diggy had asked.

"Because Ronald will do anything to keep McGann safe."

"Who's McGann?" Stick asked. "His brother? His father?"

"No," Corbin said. "Shifty McGann is Ronald's lover."

Diggy gave him a funny look. At first, he considered saying something negative about two men being in love, but then decided against it. He had been taught to believe homosexuality was a sin, but his views had evolved over the years. Who the hell was he to judge anyone for anything? He figured if someone found true love, they were lucky. Stick had tried to explain this to Stick about his son Jimmy. "Who gives a shit who he loves?" he'd asked. "It don't affect you none, and it makes him happy. You don't have to understand it. You just have to accept it. If something makes him happy, and if you love him, then it should make *you* happy." That acceptance had been hard for Stick, but he'd eventually come around to it. It had been too late by then, but he'd finally gotten it.

Stick thought about saying something too, but then remembered what he'd learned from Jimmy. The things Stick had been taught growing up were wrong. What society had said back then was wrong. Love was love, and that's all there was to it, so Stick kept his mouth shut.

Corbin left them at the Sherwood Hotel, telling them no one could ever know he'd been complicit in their kidnapping McGann. He said he would go back to Donaldson and tell him they had taken him captive and he'd escaped. Diggy and Stick agreed to this, told him thank you and so long, and walked inside the building. There was no one inside to assist them, so Diggy wondered aloud, "How the hell we gon' know what apartment he's in?"

Stick pondered this but could think of no good answer. Seeing no other way to locate McGann, they were forced to wait inside the building's entrance for someone to come along that they could ask. They waited and waited, waiting for what felt like an eternity, but no one ever stepped out of the apartments or entered the building. Finally, they decided it was time to give up the ghost and just knock on doors and ask the tenants.

Stick knocked on the first door. He turned to Diggy and asked, "Why am I always the one knocking on doors?"

"'Cause you a control freak. You wanna control everything."

"That's not true," Stick said just before the door opened. When it did, there was an old Jewish man with big yellow teeth. "Yes?"

Stick reached out his hand for the old man to shake. But the old man did not shake his hand. Instead, he looked at Stick's hand like he'd been offered a handful of dog shit.

The old man squinted, trying to figure out who they were. Then he looked down at the katana Stick was carrying.

"Why do you have a sword?" the old man asked. "Are you here to kill me?"

"Not hardly," Diggy said. "We tryin' ta find someone."

"Shifty McGann," Stick said. "Do you know him?"

The old man eyed them suspiciously. "What do you want with him?"

Diggy leaned forward, about to get angry, but Stick piped up. "He's a friend of ours."

The old man's look of suspicion became even more suspicious. "I doubt that."

"What the hell's that supposed to mean?" Diggy asked.

The old man pointed at Diggy's chest. "What it means is, if this man was such a good friend, he would have told you his apartment number." He stared at them with a smirk, daring them to continue the charade.

It was Stick who ended up losing his cool, and he lunged forward and grabbed the old bastard's arms by their shirt sleeves, shoving him inside the apartment. The old man flailed backwards, waving his arms comically. As he was regaining his balance, Stick stepped in toward him. Diggy closed the door.

Stick was pointing at the old man now. "Why can't you be helpful and just tell us what we want to know? Why do you have to be a dick about it?"

The old man stared at him with an expression of defiance. "I don't have to do anything I do not wish to do, and I do not wish to assist you."

Diggy looked at Stick with a half grin. "This motherfucker here."

Stick stepped toward the old man, prepared to hurt him, but the irritated voice of a second old man said, *"Why don't you just tell the man what he wants to know, Jakob?"* Diggy, Stick, and Jakob all turned to see the second old man, glaring at Jakob.

"You always do this, Jakob!" he yelled. *"Always!* You make things hard when they could be easy. What's the matter with you, Jakob? Don't you like easy things?" He turned and looked at Stick. "I'm sorry. He's just an old *kibitser*, always causing problems." He leaned in toward Stick. "And believe me, I

should know. He's been causing me problems for longer than you've existed."

Jakob raised his fist in the air while staring at the second man. *"Just shut it! Shut it now!"*

The second old man ignored him. "Ask me whatever it is you gentlemen want to know, and I will tell you if I can."

"Shut it!" Jakob interjected.

"We're trying to find a man who lives in this building," Stick said. "His name is Shifty McGann."

The old man's face lit up. He raised his index finger happily. "I know this man, Shifty McGann! He is a neighbor! His apartment is down the hall!"

This angered Jakob, who repeated, "Shut it, Eli! Shut it now!"

The second man, Eli, waved for them to follow him. "Come with me," he said, turning toward the door.

Not to be outdone, Jakob yelled again. *"Shut it, Eli! I said shut it!"*

Eli ignored him, opening the door and smiling. He stepped into the hallway and looked back to make sure Diggy and Stick were following. "Just down here," he said. "Right this way."

Eli shuffled slowly down the hall. After he'd passed several doors on both sides, he stopped and pointed toward one on the left. He looked at them and smiled. "Here it is! This is your Shifty McGann!" He turned and knocked on the door.

A moment later, a large, burly man with the unmistakable look of stupidity opened the door. He looked at Eli, then at Diggy, then at Stick.

"I have brought these men to see you, Shifty McGann," Eli announced.

Shifty looked them over, trying to understand. "Who are you?"

Diggy stepped past Eli, pretending to be digging through his pocket. "Let me show you my credentials, Mr. McGann." Then, in a flash, he reached back and punched Shifty in the nose, dropping him like a sack of pig shit.

"That's who we are, bitch!" Diggy said.

"Oh, my!" said Eli, walking backwards.

Stick raised the katana blade and gave him a salute with it. "Thank you for all you've done, Eli."

Aghast, Eli turned and scurried away as quickly as he could.

CHAPTER EIGHTY-FOUR

With Shifty's hands tied behind his back with his own belt, Diggy and Stick led him through the rain toward the building that housed the Oracle. It was a good distance away, and Shifty wasn't pleased.

"When I get this belt off, I'll—"

"You ain't gon' do shit," Diggy said. "Just shut your fuckin' mouth and keep walkin', dipshit."

Shifty kept walking, but he didn't stop talking.

"I don't understand any of this," Shifty said. "Can you at least tell me what's happening?"

Stick put his arm around Shifty's shoulders. "We're taking you to see Ronald."

Shifty blinked at him. "Why are we going to see Ronald? Who are you?"

Stick grinned. "That's two questions. Which one do you want me to answer?"

"Both, either one, whichever," Shifty said. "Tell me anything, but tell me *something*. Because I don't have a clue what's happening."

"We need you to get to the Oracle," Diggy said.

"Do you have a pass?" Shifty asked. "If you don't have a pass, you won't be able to use it. Ronald can't let anyone use the Oracle without a pass."

"It just so happens that we do have a pass," Stick said.

Diggy winked at Shifty. "And it's you."

"*Me?*"

"Ronald loves you, right?" Diggy asked.

"I think so," Shifty said. "At least he'd better."

"You're our insurance policy," Diggy said.

Shifty gave him a stupid look. "I thought you said I was your pass."

Diggy turned and smacked him in the forehead with an open hand. "Dammit, man, you're both. You're our insurance policy *and* our ticket, okay? Why you gotta ask so many questions?"

Shifty looked down and they could see he was trying to work this out in his head. Then he looked up at Diggy. "How am I your pass? I don't understand."

Stick said, "If Ronald wants to see you live—" Stick held the katana blade up to remind Shifty he was wielding it. "—then he'll do what we say, and he'll let Diggy go back to Earth."

Shifty looked concerned now. "I don't think that's gonna work. Ronald is real particular about this stuff. A stickler for the rules."

"I got a question," Diggy said.

Shifty turned to look at him.

"Who the hell is Ronald?" Diggy said. "And how is it that he controls the Oracle? Did he invent it or somethin'?"

Shifty shook his head. "Oh no," he said. "The Oracle has always existed. It's been here as long as Hades has been around."

"So where does Ronald fit into that?" Stick asked.

"It's his job to control the Oracle," Shifty explained. "There are several of them, you know. The Oracle Ronald controls is just one of many."

"Who hired Ronald?" Diggy asked. "Who gave him his job?"

"The big man," Shifty said. "The boss of all bosses."

Diggy raised an eyebrow. "Who the hell's that?"

"Satan," Shifty said. "Who else would it be?"

CHAPTER EIGHTY-FIVE

Diggy and Stick made Shifty knock on the door, with Stick just standing out of sight to his left. Stick had the katana raised overhead, ready to slice into Shifty's head should the need arise. Shifty looked nervous. He glanced over at Diggy, standing to his right. Diggy whispered angrily, *"Keep your eyes on the damn door!"*

The door opened, and Horsecock appeared, looking Shifty up and down.

"What you want?" Horsecock asked.

"I'm here to see Ronald," Shifty said.

Horsecock stood there for a long moment, considering this. "What is password?"

Shifty thought about it, trying to remember. "Simon says?"

Horsecock stared at him with suspicion. "That old password." Then he said, "You stay. I go get." He closed the door.

"You doin' good," Diggy whispered.

"Academy Award-level performance," Stick said, still holding the katana over his head, ready to strike.

"You best keep that shit up, unless you want Sticky there to slice your head like a melon," Diggy said.

Shifty stared at the door, saying nothing.

A moment later, it opened again, and Ronald filled the doorway.

"What's up, man?" Ronald said, seeing only Shifty.

Stick emerged and grabbed Shifty, putting his arm around his neck. He held the sword up to Shifty's throat with his other hand.

Diggy stepped out, revealing his presence.

"What is all this?" Ronald asked. He looked at Shifty. "You okay, man?"

"So far."

Ronald looked back and forth between the captors. "What's up, guys?"

"I need you to let my friend use the Oracle," Stick said.

Ronald shook his head. "No," he said. "There's no way I can do that. Not without a pass. I don't suppose you fellas have one?"

"We got a fuckin' pass," Diggy said. Stick tightened his arm around Shifty's throat.

"What does that mean?" Ronald asked, simultaneously looking confused, nervous, and scared.

"If you don't let us use the Oracle, I'll re-kill Shifty," Stick said.

Ronald's eyes grew wide. "You'd...*you'd do that?*"

"I would," Stick said solemnly.

Ronald looked at Stick with an expression of sadness. "I thought we kind of connected when you were here. I thought we were friends."

"Sorry," Stick said. "This is business. It's not personal."

"That's what everyone says, isn't it?"

Shifty looked at Ronald with pleading eyes. "Please get this idiot off me."

Diggy grinned and looked at Stick. "Ol Shifty here's only known you for a little while, and he already knows you an idiot."

Stick, one arm around Shifty's neck and the other holding the katana to his throat, said, "If I had a free hand, I'd flip you off, Dig. Just know that, in my head, I'm flipping you off right now."

Ronald said. "Why don't you let Shifty go and we can talk

237

about this like civilized adults."

"We ain't civilized," Diggy said.

"I see can that."

"Ain't you at least gon' invite us in?"

Ronald shrugged, turning to usher them inside.

"You best not try no stupid shit," Diggy warned.

Diggy led the way, giving Ronald dagger eyes as he passed. Stick and Shifty—Shifty still in a headlock—followed. Ronald closed the door behind them.

Suddenly, Horsecock emerged from a side room, carrying a short sword. Horsecock and Diggy came face-to-face. Neither was expecting to see the other, so both were caught off guard. Diggy's reflexes were quicker, and he used all his weight to slam the small man into the door frame. Horsecock let out a yelp. Diggy grabbed his hand and smashed it against the wall, forcing Horsecock to drop the sword. Diggy threw a hard elbow into his throat, smashing him against the door frame again. He kept his elbow pressed against Horsecock's throat until he passed out, falling to the floor.

Ronald looked at Horsecock and shrugged. "So much for security, I guess."

Panting and winded, Diggy said, "Your security sucks."

With Ronald's assistance, they found a storage room. Diggy dragged the unconscious Chinese man inside. Panting, Diggy lamented, "It woulda been easier just to re-kill him." Diggy turned to Ronald. "You got a key for this door?"

Ronald shook his head. "I don't think there is one."

"Well, hell," Diggy muttered.

"Just grab that table down the hall, and slide it in front of the door," Stick said.

"You think it's heavy enough to keep him in there?"

"I think so," Ronald said.

"Nobody asked you," Stick said.

"So keep your fuckin' mouth shut," Diggy said.

"I don't like you talking to Ronald like that," Shifty said.

Diggy looked at him with a crazy look. "Ain't nobody asked you neither, so you'd be wise to shut the fuck up too!"

CHAPTER EIGHTY-SIX

The three of them walked down the many stairs to get to the Oracle. When they reached the door where the Oracle was kept, it was closed.

Stick looked at Ronald. "Go ahead and do that fancy knock."

Ronald did, and the door opened a few seconds later. The large black man with the big scar and the dead eye stayed behind the door. He didn't even look out to see them, since he trusted the knock. Sword in hand, Diggy flung himself into the door as hard as he could, knocking it back against the guard. The big man fell to the floor but managed to keep hold of his hatchet. Diggy tried to rush him with his sword before he could get up, but the man saw him coming and was back on his feet in seconds.

If the guard wondered who they were, he didn't say anything about it. He just went to work fighting Diggy. As Stick watched, he felt Shifty move the slightest bit. Worried he might try to break free, Stick pulled the katana blade closer to his Adam's apple.

The guard charged at Diggy with his hatchet raised, but Diggy was unfazed. When the guard reached him, Diggy moved out of the way, and the big man crashed into a big computer-looking machine. But this didn't seem to hurt him, and he didn't pause. He turned to face Diggy in a flash, his hatchet raised and ready. But now it was Diggy's turn to rush at him, and he held the tip of Horsecock's sword out like they were jousting. Scarface

240

moved out to the side the way Diggy had, and the tip of Diggy's sword collided with the giant computer.

Before Diggy could recover, the guard charged at him again. Diggy pulled back the arm holding the sword and managed to block him with the grip. Although the guard had the hatchet up, the sword's grip smashing into his nose was enough to discombobulate him, causing him to stagger. In that instant, Diggy twirled free and brought the blade up from his side, ramming it into the man's chest.

The guard pulled away, his eyes big. The sword was still protruding from his chest. He looked down at the sword and tried to pull it free. Before he could accomplish this, Diggy threw a hard right into his throat, cracking his windpipe. The guard staggered backwards, his hands around his throat. He was making a wheezing sound. Diggy grabbed the grip of the sword and pulled the blade out of his chest. The guard could do nothing, and his hands remained clutched around his neck. His eyes were still big and his face was turning purple.

That was the expression on his face when Diggy rammed the end of the sword through his head. The guard stood there, wobbling on gelatin legs. He tried to take a step, apparently figured out he was dead, and fell hard, face-first onto the cement floor.

"Damn," Ronald said. "Mick was a nice guy."

Out of breath and exhausted, Diggy said, "Fuck Mick."

"Let's cut the chit-chat and get to it," Stick said.

"Put me in the chair and send me back," Diggy said.

Ronald held his palms up. "It's not that easy. I can't just send people back willy-nilly."

Diggy looked at Stick. "Cut Shifty's throat."

Ronald looked at Stick nervously. "Please don't hurt him."

"We ain't got no choice, Ronald," Diggy said. "You puttin' us in a bad position."

Ronald became animated. "You think *I'm* putting *you* in a bad position? *Do you have any fucking clue what you guys are doing to me?!"*

"It can't be helped," Stick said.

"I gotta go back," Diggy said. "It's imperative."

Ronald said, "He'll re-kill me if I send you back."

"Well," Stick said, his blade still pressed against Shifty's throat, "if you don't help us, then I re-kill Shifty."

There were tears in Ronald's eyes. He looked at Shifty. "What do I do?"

"Screw these guys," Shifty said. "Don't do it. Let them eat shit."

Ronald gazed at Shifty like he was looking at him for the last time. "No," he said. "If one of us is going to die, it's got to be me."

The two men stared at each other for a long moment, both of them weeping.

"This is quite the touching scene," Stick said. "But you need to send Diggy back *now*."

"Let me die instead of you," Shifty said.

"I got news for you two," Diggy said. "If Ronald don't send me back, both y'all motherfuckers gon' die."

Ronald exhaled a deep breath. "Alright," he said. "Let's send you home."

CHAPTER EIGHTY-SEVEN

Diggy was strapped into the chair, and Ronald was flipping switches and pressing buttons.

"Everything's going to spin for a moment," Ronald said. "If you close your eyes, it should stop you from getting sick."

Diggy sat back in the seat, all necessary head gear and electrodes attached.

"Don't do this for me," Shifty urged Ronald.

Ronald ignored him and continued flipping switches. Stick tightened his hold on Shifty, warning him, "Don't get any ideas."

Shifty didn't care about Stick or his katana. He had tears in his eyes as he uttered one last plea. "Please, Ronald. Don't do it."

Ronald looked at Shifty with sad eyes. "I've got to." He pushed the last sequence of buttons, bringing the Oracle to life. A bright light surrounded Diggy and filled the room. The computer made a loud humming sound. Diggy pressed his head back against the head rest and clasped his eyes as tightly closed as he could.

Ronald and Stick held one another's gaze. Shifty's eyes remained locked on Ronald. A moment later, the machine stopped making all the racket and Diggy fell limp with his head hanging down.

For a moment, Stick thought Diggy was dead. He worried that Ronald had re-killed him. His body tensed and he started to move, his arm still locked around Shifty's neck. "Is he okay?"

Ronald nodded, still frowning. "Yeah," he said. "He's in Kansas City now."

"Near Armourdale?" Stick asked.

"Like I told you, I can only assure that he'll be somewhere within a two-mile radius. This isn't an exact science."

"I would have thought the science would be more exact here," Stick said.

Ronald looked at him. "I would have thought you'd be less of a dick. We were both wrong, weren't we?"

CHAPTER EIGHTY-EIGHT

Diggy opened his eyes. Where was he? Following that, an even better question came to him: *who* was he?

He was sitting in a soft recliner. The legs of the chair were not extended. There was an old school floor model television in front of him. He studied it for a moment. What was he watching? It looked like *Murder She Wrote*, but maybe not. It looked boring, whatever it was. Diggy put his hands on the arms of the chair and pushed himself up. He had far less strength than he normally had. Now standing, he raised his arm and examined it. The first thing he noticed was that it was a yellowish-white arm with brown spots. The second thing he noticed was that the skin, hanging from an extremely bony arm, was as thin as paper.

Apparently he was an old man. How could he possibly kill Benny Cordella in this body? Feeling something on his face, he raised his hand and felt glasses there. He'd never worn glasses before, so this was new for him. He looked around, seeing a hallway behind him. He slowly made his way to it, making his way past a kitchen on his left. As he walked—*slowly, so slowly*—he noted a smell in the air. What was it? Then it came to him—moth balls. Christ, he really was an old man.

There were two doors ahead to his right and a third to the far left. He opened the first door he came to and found himself looking at a dusty old car (he thought it was a Buick) parked in a dark garage. He turned and walked to the second door. He opened it. It was a bathroom. He stepped inside and flipped the light switch. The light came on, and there was a dirty green sink with a lot of pill bottles scattered around it.

Diggy looked up, seeing his reflection for the first time, and he was staring at the face of a frail, eighty-something-year-old white woman with bluish-gray hair and thick, round glasses.

"Well, fuck me with a wire hanger," he muttered, staring at his new face.

This was going to complicate things.

CHAPTER EIGHTY-NINE

Standing beside Diggy's unconscious body, Ronald looked at Stick. "Why are you doing this? Couldn't you have just gotten a pass from Swearengen? He could have got you one."

"We didn't have that option," Stick said. "We're not with him anymore. He sold us out and almost got us killed."

Ronald grinned a half-hearted grin and nodded. "That sounds like him."

Stick was still holding Shifty in front of him. Shifty asked, "Are you really going to let me live?"

"If everything goes okay, and you and Ronald do what you're supposed to do, there shouldn't be any trouble," Stick said.

Ronald shrugged and rolled his eyes. "Maybe not for you guys. But me? I'm in a world of shit. Satan's gonna re-kill me at the very least." He met Stick's gaze. "Probably a lot more."

"I'm sorry," Stick said, meaning it. "There was no other way."

"At least tell me this," Ronald said. "Tell me why he had to go. Did he have the cure for cancer? Did he go to save someone he loved?"

"He went back to kill the man who sent us here."

Ronald stared at him for a long, uncomfortable moment. "So, let me get this straight. You came here and did *this*, getting me *re-killed*, all so you could get revenge?"

Stick just stared at him. There was nothing he could say.

"You guys are a couple of real dicks," Ronald said. "I hope you know that."

"I do," Stick said somberly.

At that moment, Ronald's eyes got big and his body stiffened. His head tilted upward.

"*Ronald,*" Shifty said, gasping in horror.

Stick and Shifty could only watch as Ronald's body started to shake and gyrate, his eyes open, a long string of saliva dangling from his mouth.

"He's having a seizure," Stick said.

"No," Shifty said. "This is what happens when you break the rules. He's being electrocuted. This will continue for…" He considered it, trying to think of the correct word. Finally, he said, "It'll go on for a *long* time. What would have been days, maybe weeks on Earth."

"Then what?"

"Who can say?" Shifty said sadly. "My guess is he'll be re-killed and sent to some darker, shittier place."

CHAPTER NINETY

Diggy went to the garage. He flipped the switch to turn on the light, but no light came. He pushed the button to the electric garage door opener so he could get a good look at the car and maybe find something to use as a weapon. The garage door made a grating sound as it came to life, and as it slowly raised from the ground, daylight poured into the garage and he could see the car.

It was an old, dirty, dinged all to hell white Buick LeSabre. He didn't know what year it was, but knew it was from the nineties. As he stood staring at the car, the garage door came to a loud, jarring halt halfway up. He pushed the button again, and the garage door started moving down. He pushed it a third time, and it went up but got stuck in the same position as before.

Now a new problem occurred to him—the car keys. He had no idea where they were. He hoped he would find them dangling in the ignition, but he wasn't optimistic. He (as the old woman) hobbled to the driver's-side door and opened it. The door much harder to pull open than he'd expected. In the old woman's body, Diggy was far weaker than he'd ever been. Once he had the car door open, he peered inside, and could, thankfully, see the keys hanging in the ignition.

Thank you, sweet Jesus, he thought.

There was no time to celebrate this minor victory as there

were other things to do. The first was to find a suitable weapon. Diggy made his way around the car, searching the cobweb-covered garage for something he could use—a hammer, hatchet, he would have killed for a pistol—but found nothing. Looking around, he spotted a red metal toolbox on the floor ahead. He slowly shuffled toward it. When he reached it, he realized getting down to the floor to open it could be tricky. His legs were wobbly and his balance wasn't great. He worried he might fall trying to lower himself, possibly breaking a hip. Old people were highly susceptible to broken hips, and if he busted one now, the mission would be over. Diggy pressed his hand against the wall to steady himself and lowered his body slowly. He flipped the latch on the toolbox, and his back hurt immediately. He could feel his legs wobbling. He pulled the toolbox lid open and peered inside, finding only a pair of pliers, a tire pressure gauge, and a Philips-head screwdriver. With a sigh, he took the screwdriver.

It took him a while to raise himself back up to an erect position (or what passed for an erect position in the old woman's body). He made his way around the car, and then climbed in behind the steering wheel. He looked over and saw the old woman's purse sitting in the passenger's seat.

He turned the key and started the Buick, which sounded surprisingly good for its age. Remembering that the garage door was still stuck halfway down, he'd have to drive through it, scraping the roof of the car. Diggy shifted into reverse and stomped the gas, and the old Buick shot backwards, catching the hanging door and dragging it along. As the Buick rocketed toward the street, it shed the detached garage door. Diggy stomped the brake just as the Buick reached the street, and the car came to a screeching halt.

CHAPTER NINETY-ONE

Stick still had his arm locked around Shifty's neck, and the two men watched Ronald's body, still standing, convulse as electricity coursed through it. There was a pungent odor in the air, and they knew Ronald had soiled himself.

Shifty was wailing now, and Stick was holding him up. His katana blade was still raised but was now at Shifty's midsection. Shifty showed no signs he was going to attempt an escape.

Recognizing he and Diggy had caused Shifty's pain, Stick felt bad. He thought he should say something, but he wasn't sure what. So he said softly, "It's going to be okay." This made Shifty cry harder.

Stick was contemplating what else he could say when Horsecock walked in. Seeing movement in his peripheral vision, Stick turned and saw the small man. He was carrying a spear.

"Where the fuck did you get a spear?" Stick blurted. He hadn't meant to say it, but the words just popped out.

Horsecock pointed the tip of the spear at Stick. "I come kill you!"

Stick grinned. "You've got to pick one, pal. Are you gonna cum, or are you gonna kill me?"

The weeping Shifty giggled despite himself. Horsecock didn't understand, so he just stared at them in confusion.

"What the hell are you going to do with a spear?" Stick asked.

Stick started to push Shifty away so he could fight Horsecock, but the Chinese man hurled his spear at the exact same moment. Stick could see it flying toward Shifty, almost in slow motion. Stick started to yell, but he couldn't get anything out before the spear impaled Shifty through the neck.

Stick didn't know why he cared about Horsecock re-killing Shifty—maybe it was just the pent-up anger he felt from all the crazy shit that had happened recently—but in that moment, he was so angry that he sprung toward Horsecock. The Chinese man's eyes grew large as Stick came at him with the katana raised over his head.

Horsecock shielded his eyes with his forearm and screamed, *"No!"* as the blade of the katana swooped down toward his head. The blade sliced its way deep into the top of his skull, stopping between his eyes. Stick pulled the blade out and watched Horsecock drop dead.

Stick turned to Shifty. He was still alive. His eyes fluttered, and his body convulsed similar to Ronald's a few feet away. Half the spear protruded from each side of his neck like a shish kabob. *Shift kabob!* Stick hated himself for thinking this, but it was a thought he had. Stick stepped toward Shifty. The dying man lay on his side, clutching at the spear.

"I'm sorry for everything," Stick said, raising the sword over his head.

CHAPTER NINETY-TWO

After determining his location, Diggy found that he was only about a mile from Benny's home. The two neighborhoods were quite different, but sometimes a mile made a dramatic difference. The old woman's neighborhood was fairly rundown. It had probably been a nice middle-class neighborhood fifty years ago, but now it was a slightly below average neighborhood populated by old people, janitors, and fast food and box store employees. Benny's neighborhood, on the other hand, was a gated community filled with giant houses costing millions.

An older Buick LeSabre would stick out like a dead man's dick. The help probably drove nicer cars.

Once he located Benny's big, gaudy McMansion, Diggy turned into the circular drive and parked in front of the entrance. There was a big, stupid-looking goon on guard outside, smoking a cigarette. Diggy grabbed the old woman's purse. When he did, he saw the name "Emily" embroidered on it. Well, now he knew what the woman's name was. Sorry, Emily, he thought as he walked up the short walkway toward the goon.

The guy looked at him. "Can I help you with something?"

Diggy smiled a nice old lady smile. "Hello there, young man. I'm here to see Benjamin Cordella."

No one called Benny "Benjamin," and Diggy wasn't even sure he really was a Benjamin, but Diggy thought it a nice touch. It sounded like something a nice old woman might say.

253

The guy furrowed his brow. "Benjamin, huh?"

"Yes," Diggy said, nodding happily.

"And who are you?"

"My name is Emily. I'm friends with Benjamin's mother."

The guy stood there for a moment staring at him. Then he nodded and knocked three knocks in quick succession. The door opened almost immediately, and a big bodybuilder-looking asshole wearing a Hawaiian shirt appeared. He looked at Diggy and then at the other asshole.

"Old lady," Asshole #1 said, as if Bodybuilder Fuck couldn't see that for himself. "Says she wants to talk to *Benjamin*." His voice was light, almost slipping into a chuckle. "Says she's friends with his mom."

Bodybuilder Fuck squinted at Diggy. "I thought his mom was dead."

Was she dead? Diggy didn't know, but he maintained his nice old woman smile. "Yes, but there's something she wanted me to share with Benjamin."

Bodybuilder Fuck moved his head back on his shoulders and blinked. Then he nodded. "Okay," he said, looking at Asshole #1. "I'll go inside and ask." Then he took another look at the person he believed to be an old woman, and smirked, saying, "*Benjamin*." He turned and was about to go inside, but then he stopped and turned. "What did you say your name was?"

"Emily."

"Emily what?"

Diggy wanted to say "Emily mind-your-own-fucking-business-and-go-get-Benny-you-punk-motherfucker," but instead he said, "Emily Dickinson" He wasn't sure where the name had come from, but he was happy he'd pulled it in the spur of the moment.

"Okay, Emily Dickinson," Bodybuilder Fuck said. "Wait here."

Bodybuilder Fuck wandered off, leaving the door open. Asshole #1 looked at Diggy. "You knew Benny's mama, huh?"

Diggy nodded. "Oh yes, I knew her for years."

Diggy knew what the next question would be, and it worried him. He would ask where he knew her from, and then Diggy would have to spin some shit that might or might not fly. Lucky for him, the guy took a drag on his cigarette and looked down the street.

Then he looked at Diggy. "Where'd you know—"

At that moment, Bodybuilder Fuck reappeared and waved him in. "Boss says it's okay."

Diggy looked at Asshole #1 finishing his cigarette and said, "You have a nice day, young man."

"You too."

Diggy winked. "Oh, I will."

CHAPTER NINETY-THREE

Bodybuilder Fuck led Diggy through a series of hallways, past a lot of rooms with goons in them. There were three men playing cards in one. There was reggaeton music playing in another. In a third, there were a couple of muscle-bound fucks playing pool. The house was sparsely decorated and what there was was gaudy as hell. Diggy didn't know the first thing about art, but the large paintings on the walls looked like they'd been created by a small child who'd filled his asshole with paint and then shit-sprayed it onto canvas.

Finally, they reached a large room with a fireplace, more gaudy shit-sprayed paintings on the walls, and several pieces of plush-looking white furniture. Benny was sitting his big Kingpin-looking ass on a white couch facing a giant-screen television. He had a video game controller in his hand. When Diggy and Bodybuilder Fuck entered the room, Benny set the controller down and looked up.

"It don't matter none," Benny said. "I suck at this game anyway."

He looked at Diggy and smiled the respectful pretend-nice smile you gave to an elderly woman. "Hello," he said, putting his hand out. He looked at Bodybuilder Fuck and waved him off. "I'll call you if I need you." Diggy hobbled toward Benny and shook his hand. He considered going for the screwdriver in his purse at that moment but opted to wait. There wasn't adequate time to go for it and do it right. "Can I sit beside you?" Diggy asked.

This seemed to catch Benny off guard. He looked at the empty chairs around the room. Then he looked at Diggy uncomfortably. "Uh, sure. Have a seat," he said as he patted the couch cushion beside him.

As Diggy sat, Benny said with genuine curiosity, "I understand you knew my mother."

Diggy knew there was no time to fuck around. He couldn't risk a hundred goons coming in or him suddenly being sucked back to Hades before he'd done the deed. He set the purse on his lap. "There's something she wanted you to have, Benjamin." Benny watched Diggy rifle through the purse, acting like he was looking for something.

Diggy wrapped his hand around the screwdriver's plastic handle. When he went to pull it out, it snagged on something inside the purse, and he fumbled taking it out. Then the screwdriver was out and in front of him, and Benny stared at it with a look of bewilderment.

"My mother wanted me to have...a screwdriver?"

Benny's eyes raised from the screwdriver to meet Diggy's eyes, and he asked, "Can I look at it?"

"Have a close look," Diggy said as his arm shot forward—not with the power he would have liked, but *enough* power—and he rammed the screwdriver's pointed tip into Benny's right eye. Benny screamed, tried to stand but couldn't. He raised his hands to the wound. In that time, Diggy slid the screwdriver out and jammed it hard—*harder this time*—through Benny's other eye. This time he buried the screwdriver all the way to the hilt.

As Benny was screaming and thrashing against the no-longer-white couch, Diggy said, *"You said you was gonna poke out my daddy's eyes, you fuck!"*

Benny's goons arrived just as their boss did the last bit of his thrashing.

Diggy turned and looked at them. Bodybuilder Fuck stood

there looking stupid. "What the hell?"

Diggy flipped them all off, chuckling. *"Fuck all you inbred cunt motherfuckers! This is for Diggy and Stick!"*

Diggy didn't see which goon fired first, but he felt the bullet burning into his right shoulder. That was followed by a cacophony of gunshots, one of them catching him in the head. Although Diggy was aware he'd been shot in the head, it didn't hurt. Everything went black, and Diggy slipped off into the warm darkness.

CHAPTER NINETY-FOUR

Stick was standing over Diggy, waiting for him to return. Diggy opened his eyes, but he didn't speak.

Stick said, "You okay, Dig?"

"Could you tell Ronald to unstrap me?"

"Ronald's indisposed at the moment."

"Okay then, could *you* unstrap this shit?"

Stick nodded and went to work unstrapping and unhooking everything.

"You're okay?" Stick asked again.

"I'm okay," Diggy said. "But the old woman…she's dead."

"Old woman?"

"I'll tell you about it later. I don't wanna talk about it right now. But Benny's dead too in case you was wonderin'."

"He is?"

"I got his ass good."

Once Diggy was free of all straps and electrodes, he looked down at the dead bodies on the floor. "Looks like you boys had quite a party while I was gone."

"Honestly, it was a pretty shit party."

"No strippers and blow?"

Stick shook his head. "Sadly, no."

Diggy stood and surveyed the room, now able to see Ronald standing there convulsing behind him. He looked at the bodies again.

"I got one question, though," Diggy said.

"What's that?"

"Where the fuck did that spear come from?"

CHAPTER NINETY-FIVE

Diggy and Stick were sitting at a table inside a small, dim pub a few blocks from the Oracle.

"Where are we going to stay tonight?" Stick asked.

Mentally exhausted, Diggy said, "A hotel, I guess."

"We need to figure out what our next move is."

Diggy met his gaze. "My next move is to find a bed and go to sleep. I'm so tired I can't think straight."

"You'll tell me about Benny and the old woman and whatever the hell else when you wake up?"

"I will."

"What about Swearengen?" Stick said. "We've still got to pay him back."

"I can only handle gettin' revenge on one bastard at a time."

Stick chuckled and took a drink.

Diggy looked at him wearily. "Here's a thought for ya, by the way. Has it occurred to you that at some point the now-deceased Benny Cordella is gonna show up here?"

"Shit," Stick said, looking down at the table. "I hadn't even considered that."

"The good news is, we get to kill him all over again."

"I call dibs," Stick said.

"That's fine," Diggy said. "Right now, I just wanna get some sleep."

"You remember those paperbacks I liked to read back home?"

"Them shitty westerns?"

Stick nodded. "One and the same."

"What about 'em?"

Stick grinned. "If we were in one of those paperbacks, they would say we still have a few loose ends to tie up."

"Are any of them books part of a series?"

Stick nodded. "Some of them, yeah."

"What happens if there's still loose ends in a book that's part of a series?"

"They tie up the loose ends in the next book."

Diggy downed the rest of his whiskey. Then he said, "We'll get around to them loose ends. After all, we're here for eternity."

ANDY RAUSCH is the author of many fiction and nonfiction books. His novels include *American Trash*, *Layla's Score*, and *Savage Brooklyn*. He is also the editor of the anthology *Dead-End Jobs: A Hitman Anthology*.

On the following pages are a few
more great titles from the
Down & Out Books publishing family.

For a complete list of books and to
sign up for our newsletter,
go to DownAndOutBooks.com.

Mickey Finn: 21ˢᵗ Century Noir
Michael Bracken, Editor

Down & Out Books
December 2021
978-1-64396-242-9

Mickey Finn: 21st Century Noir, Volume 2, second volume of the hard-hitting series, is a crime-fiction cocktail that will knock readers into a literary stupor.

Contributors—Trey R. Barker, John Bosworth, Michael Bracken, Scott Bradfield, S.M. Fedor, Nils Gilbertson, J.D. Graves, James A. Hearn, Janice Law, Hugh Lessig, Gabe Morran, Rick Ollerman, Josh Pachter, Robert Petyo, Stephen D. Rogers, Albert Tucher, Joseph S. Walker, Sam Wiebe, and Stacy Woodson—push hard against the boundaries of crime fiction, driving their work into places short crime fiction doesn't often go, into a world where the mean streets seem gentrified by comparison and happy endings are the exception, not the rule.

Razing Stakes
The De La Cruz Case Files
TG Wolff

Down & Out Books
February 2022
978-1-64396-245-0

Colin McHenry is out for his regular run when an SUV crosses into his path, crushing him. Within hours of the hit-skip, Cleveland Homicide Detective Jesus De La Cruz finds the vehicle in the owner's garage, who's on vacation three time zones away. The suspects read like a list out of a textbook: the jilted fiancée, the jealous coworker, the overlooked subordinate, the dirty client.

Motives, opportunities, and alibis don't point in a single direction. In these mysteries, Cruz has to think laterally, yanking down the curtain to expose the master minding the strings.

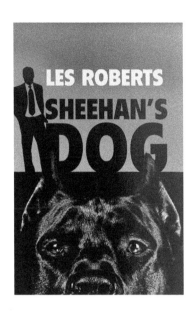

Sheehan's Dog
Les Roberts

Down & Out Books
February 2022
978-1-64396-247-4

Former Irish mafia hitman Brock Sheehan lives quietly on a boat fifty miles from Cleveland. When his long-lost nephew, Linus Callahan, tracks him down and asks him for assistance, he agrees to help. A few days earlier, the nephew got into a bar argument with a multimillion-dollar basketball player just released from prison for running a high-level dog-fighting ring. Then the athlete is murdered, and Linus becomes the Cleveland police department's "person of interest."

Investigating the athlete's former dogfight ring, Brock winds up with a pit bull of his own, which he names Conor. And eventually, with Conor's instincts, he discovers and turns over to the police the real killer of the dog-killer turned sports legend.

Bad Guy Lawyer
Chuck Marten

Down & Out Books
March 2022
978-1-64396-249-8

The only time Guy McCann stops talking is when he's downing scotch. Guy was a hot-shot attorney for the West Coast mafia until he got cold feet and split town, earning a target on his head. Now he's lying low in Las Vegas, giving back-room legal advice to second-rate crooks while pining over his old girlfriend Blair, a working girl with a razor wit and zero inhibitions.

When Blair is committed to a psychiatric ward, Guy is drawn back to the dangerous underworld of Los Angeles. Next thing he knows, Blair has escaped from the hospital and Guy's former mafia associates are on her trail, with Guy caught in the cross-fire.